Emmeline and the Plucky Pup

megan rix

PUFFIN

PUFFIN BOOKS

UK | USA | Canada | Ireland | Australia
India | New Zealand | South Africa

Puffin Books is part of the Penguin Random House group of companies
whose addresses can be found at global.penguinrandomhouse.com.

www.penguin.co.uk
www.puffin.co.uk
www.ladybird.co.uk

Penguin
Random House
UK

First published 2018

001

Set in 13/20 pt Baskerville MT
Typeset by Jouve (UK), Milton Keynes
Printed in Great Britain by Clays Ltd, St Ives plc

A CIP catalogue record for this book is available from the British Library

ISBN: 978-0-141-38570-9

All correspondence to:
Puffin Books
Penguin Random House Children's
80 Strand, London WC2R 0RL

MIX
Paper from
responsible sources
FSC® C018179

Penguin Random House is committed to a
sustainable future for our business, our readers
and our planet. This book is made from Forest
Stewardship Council® certified paper.

'Fall down seven times, get up eight'

Japanese proverb

'We are fighting for a time when every little girl born into the world will have an equal chance with her brothers.'

Emmeline Pankhurst,

The Suffragette, 27 February 1914

Prologue

1906

'Alfie, Alfie, wake up!' a voice hissed into the darkness.

Half asleep, Alfie pulled the threadbare blanket over his head and wriggled down further in his lumpy bed. Around him in the dormitory, another hundred boys snored and snuffled as they slept, tired out from the long workhouse day. They were woken at six o'clock in the morning, did lessons till noon and then worked all afternoon, with only gruel and watery stew or bread for each meal, and went to bed at eight o'clock. Usually work meant putting the heads on pins, or breaking stones into little bits. Sometimes Alfie folded sheets that had been pressed by the mangle in the laundry and once he'd helped to peel hundreds and hundreds of potatoes. But this afternoon he'd been given a new, much more fun job.

'Alfie, take Sniffer for a walk,' Matron had said.

'Me?' Alfie wasn't used to dogs and had never walked one before. He'd looked down at Matron's elderly Yorkshire terrier, which could be very growly at people he wasn't fond of.

The two of them set off round the workhouse yard, with Alfie gently holding Sniffer's lead. This afternoon Sniffer didn't growl even once.

'Sniffer does seem to like you,' Matron said, as Sniffer rolled over on to his back and Alfie gave him a tummy rub. 'And he doesn't like many people, as you know.'

Alfie liked Sniffer too and hoped he could take him for another walk in the morning.

'Alfie – it's me!' A hand shook his shoulder and gave him a gentle flick on his sleepy shaved head.

Only one person flicked him like that.

Alfie's eyes flew open. 'What are you doing here, Daisy?' he whispered into the darkness. 'You'll be for it if you're caught.'

'Get up.' His big sister pulled the blanket from his bed.

It was freezing in the dormitory and Alfie had put all his day clothes back on over his nightshirt for warmth, even though he knew how much trouble he'd be in if Matron caught him wearing them. Daisy was wearing her grey workhouse dress and long white apron.

'You shouldn't be h–' he said.

3

Daisy pressed her finger to his lips.

'*Shush!* We're leaving. Right now.'

Alfie gulped. They couldn't just leave the workhouse, not without permission. What if Matron or the governor or the police caught them? They could be sent to prison or brought back to the workhouse and punished. Alfie didn't want to be locked in a little room by himself or beaten with a stick, and he certainly didn't want to be given less food to eat. There was barely enough to stop his belly from rumbling as it was.

'Come on.' Daisy grabbed his wrist and pulled him up.

'We could get sent to prison . . .'

'Sssh!'

Alfie pushed his bare feet into his wooden clogs and wrapped the blanket around his skinny shoulders. He didn't have a coat and he wasn't leaving the blanket behind, even though all of the boys in the dormitory knew what had happened to the other boys who'd tried to escape and been caught by the police. Not only had those boys been sent to prison but they were given even longer prison sentences because they'd dared to escape wearing *stolen* workhouse clothes.

Daisy was already making her way soundlessly past the sleeping boys, some of them crammed two or three to a narrow bed. Alfie tried to catch up with her, but one of his clogs slipped off and landed with a *clonk* on the floor. He froze with fear. The noise must have woken someone up! They'd be caught and then . . . well, Alfie didn't like to think about that.

Daisy crept back to him, picked up his clog, then took off the one that was on his other foot. She put her finger to her lips and tiptoed to the dormitory door, with Alfie creeping after her. He was so scared he had to put his hands over his mouth to stop his teeth from chattering.

Daisy had left her own clogs in the corridor outside. She picked them up but didn't put them back on. Alfie's feet were freezing. They made little slapping sounds on the stone floor as he ran after his sister.

He'd often seen Daisy and the other girls on their hands and knees scrubbing the long corridors with hard brushes and soapy water. Matron said it had to be done every day to keep the dirt away. She didn't like dirt. It was why he'd had to have his head shaved. 'Fleas and sneezes spread diseases,' she'd told him, as he watched locks of his dark hair landing on the floor and a small girl quickly gathered them up.

There were lots of sneezes and diseases at the workhouse, as well as fleas.

The stairs were just ahead of them. Downstairs was the room where Matron slept, with her name written on the door. Alfie stopped at the top of the stairs but Daisy took his hand and squeezed it.

'We have to,' she whispered.

The moon was shining through the big window on the landing and he saw that she looked as frightened as he felt.

He looked back along the corridor. Maybe they should go back? Daisy squeezed his hand again.

Alfie nodded but dared not speak. He held on to the polished wooden bannister and stepped as softly as he could. At the bottom he tiptoed across the tiled entrance hall after Daisy.

They were nearly past Matron's door when a dog started yapping and Alfie almost jumped out of his skin.

Sniffer!

The yapping was followed by a great hacking, heaving cough from inside the room.

People were always getting sick at the workhouse. Some of them, like Alfie's mum, didn't get better and died from it. Now it sounded like Matron was sick too. But she was also awake!

Sniffer barked again, then he whined and Alfie heard the little dog scratching at the door.

Daisy grabbed Alfie's arm and dragged him down a corridor leading to the dining hall and kitchens. She stopped so suddenly Alfie bumped into her.

'This way,' she said, pushing up a sash window and climbing out.

After a quick look behind him, Alfie followed her.

Now they were in the yard where Alfie had taken Sniffer for a walk that afternoon. He'd never been out here at night and he moved closer to Daisy. Why had she brought him here? It wasn't safe. The yard was surrounded on three sides by red brick walls. Alfie stared up at them. Had they been seen from one of the windows? Was someone standing there looking out? Or maybe someone was already on their way, running down the stairs to drag them back.

Alfie pulled his blanket over his head to hide his face.

In the fourth wall were the massive wooden gates of the workhouse. They were guarded day and night by a fierce man with a big stick. He lived in a little hut next to the gates. What if he came out? What if he caught them? Alfie didn't want the gatekeeper to swing his stick at him or Daisy.

'Stay in the shadows,' Daisy told him, as they edged their way round the yard until they came to a small side door.

She pulled a large key from the pocket of her apron, turned it in the lock, swiftly lifted the latch, and the next moment they were out in the street.

Alfie looked at the workhouse behind him. They were out. Really out. He'd been at the Manchester workhouse since he was three and never been out of it before at night. He swallowed hard and tried not to think about what would happen if they were caught.

Daisy pulled a screwed-up piece of paper from her apron pocket.

'What's that?' Alfie asked.

'A map,' she told him, as she peered at it under a gas light.

'To where?'

'To Mrs Pankhurst's.'

'Who's Mrs Pankhurst?'

But Daisy didn't answer. She put t[...]
back in her pocket and pointed to the tall iron
gates across the cobbled street.

Alfie gasped. 'Not the cemetery! We can't
go in there.'

'You're not scared?' Daisy hissed scornfully.
'We've got a lot more to be frightened of from
real-life living people than from any ghosts!'

But Alfie *was* scared and he really didn't
want to go into the cemetery – especially
not at night. A drop of rain landed on his face
and then one fell on his hand. He hoped
the rain would keep the cemetery ghosts
away.

'If the workhouse gatekeeper comes looking
for us, he won't think to look in there, will he?'
Daisy said. 'The cemetery's not that big – if
we run as fast as we can, we'll be through it in
no time. Here, I'll hold your hand.'

Alfie sighed and squeezed through a gap in the padlocked gates after Daisy.

'Run!'

It wasn't easy running in clogs but Alfie moved so fast they didn't have a chance to slip off. He was gasping so hard it felt like his heart was going to burst by the time they reached the other gate.

Daisy clutched her stomach and leant over, drawing in big breaths of freezing night air.

An owl hooted as it flew overhead and they both jumped in fear and then laughed with relief.

'Just an owl.'

'Now where?' Alfie asked Daisy.

'Down Nell Lane,' she said, peering at her map, although Alfie didn't think she could see it properly now it was drizzling with rain.

They headed down Nell Lane and then along the banks of Chorlton Brook, where there were no street lamps and it was very dark.

Alfie's feet and legs were soon soaked in the long wet grass.

'Is it much further to Mrs Pankhurst's?' he wanted to know when they reached Sandy Lane. 'These clogs are rubbing the skin off my feet.'

They'd been walking for over an hour.

'This is the quickest way,' Daisy told him, as they headed into Ivy Green woods. 'One of the old ladies, Mary Dingle, drew the map to Mrs Pankhurst's house for me. She said we should always keep the river Mersey on our left.'

Alfie listened for the sound of running water. He couldn't swim and he didn't want to end up in the river!

Suddenly he heard someone groaning and icy fingers of terror ran down his spine.

'Daisy –' he started to say.

Daisy let out a great scream as a cow came running out of the bushes straight for her.

Not groaning but lowing!

The cow stopped dead and stared at them with its huge eyes. Alfie had never been close to a cow before but he wasn't frightened. He went to stroke it but the cow backed off and then turned the other way.

'I wasn't really scared,' Daisy said, as they headed onwards.

'I know,' Alfie told her.

Soon they'd left the countryside behind and were back on the cobblestone streets. It started to rain more heavily and Alfie and Daisy huddled together under the workhouse blanket, but they were soaked through in no time.

Just as Alfie was thinking he couldn't go any further, Daisy turned into a wide street lined with dark houses. Alfie caught a glimpse of the sign: Nelson Street. Daisy pulled him along faster, peering urgently at the house numbers, until finally they stopped at number 62. Daisy marched up to the front door and pulled on the brass bell pull.

Before long it was opened by a young woman wearing a thick dressing gown over her nightclothes, with her hair in white ribbon curlers. She stared at them through the rain.

'Are you here to see Mother?' she asked doubtfully, stepping back so they could come in.

'Yes,' a voice said from behind them. Alfie turned round and saw a thin, dark-haired young woman with clogs on her feet and a blanket-like shawl over her head to protect her from the rain. Just like them.

'Are you from the workhouse too?' Alfie asked her in the dimly lit passageway, and Daisy squeezed his hand to tell him to shush.

'No, I'm Annie Kenney, and if women get the vote there won't be any more workhouses.' She smiled at Alfie as she pulled off her damp shawl and gave it to the young woman who'd let them in. 'Thank you, Adela.'

Adela hid a tired yawn as she took the shawl.

'Mother's still up. She said she wouldn't dream of sleeping until you'd safely arrived,' she said to Annie.

Adela left them in a lamp-lit parlour with embroidered cushions on the chairs and velvet curtains at the window. There were paintings of the countryside on the walls and black-and-white photographs of people on the mantelpiece. Alfie had never been anywhere nearly as grand before. A smart, middle-aged lady with her hair in a bun was sitting in one of the chairs in front of the fire, sewing.

Annie Kenney bobbed a curtsy and Daisy quickly did the same. Alfie had no idea what he was supposed to do in the presence of a great lady, so he bowed low and then stood looking down at the rug on the floor.

'Annie.' The lady smiled.

'I'm sorry I'm so late, Mrs Pankhurst . . .'

'Call me Emmeline,' the lady said.

Annie nodded. 'I couldn't get away from Strangeways Prison until all the forms were signed. And then I hadn't expected there would be so many people at the prison gates waiting to greet me. Friends from the mill, members of the choir, my two sisters, and many suffragettes from your Women's Social and Political Union that I'd never even met before.'

Prison? Alfie thought. What had Annie been in prison for? And what was a suffragette? But he didn't dare ask.

'You're here now and that's all that matters,' the lady told her. 'I expect you're glad to get away from those dreadful, hard plank beds in prison.'

'I am indeed.' Annie nodded. 'But sad that dear Christabel's still in there. Your daughter is so brave, Mrs Pankhurst – I mean, Emmeline. She said she would gladly go through it all again. We have to keep fighting for women to have the right to vote.'

As Mrs Pankhurst stood up, her sewing slipped to the floor and Alfie hurried to pick it up and hand it back to her.

She'd been sewing the words VOTES FOR WOMEN in purple thread on a white sash with a green border.

'Thank you, dear,' Mrs Pankhurst said, as she took the sewing from him. 'What a helpful boy you've brought with you, Annie. Is he your brother?'

'Oh, no, I didn't bring him. We met on your doorstep, Mrs Pankhurst. He and his sister are from the workhouse,' Annie told her.

Alfie looked over at Daisy and bit his bottom lip. He didn't know why they were here or what was happening. All he knew was that they were going to be in terrible trouble if they were sent back to the workhouse. They'd probably be sent to prison to sleep on plank beds.

Daisy swallowed hard. 'You said you wanted to help children like us when you came to the workhouse, Mrs Pankhurst. You said you wished there was more you could do . . .'

Mrs Pankhurst nodded but she looked confused. 'That was a long time ago, when I was on the board of the Poor Law Guardians, dear. I had to give up the post in 1898 when I was widowed.'

Daisy took a deep breath. 'The other girls and women at the workhouse still remember your visits and talk about you all the time. You said how they weren't criminals or bad people just because they'd fallen on hard times and no one who lived there should feel guilty or ashamed.'

Alfie watched as a tear slipped down his sister's face. Then Daisy went on:

'Three eleven-year-old girls from the workhouse were sent to be apprenticed to the cotton mill today. They weren't even allowed to say goodbye to their parents or their brothers and sisters before they left.'

'I was sent to work at a cotton mill when I was ten and still at school,' Annie Kenney told her. She held out her hand and Alfie saw that one of her fingers was missing. 'A whirling bobbin tore it off.'

Alfie was glad he didn't have to work in a mill – yet.

'I'll be sent next and then Alfie – my brother – won't know where I've gone. Or why I've left him all alone.' Daisy's voice cracked as she spoke.

Alfie felt like crying too as his strong big sister started heaving great loud sobs from somewhere deep down inside her. It sounded as if a million tears had been bottled up tight, waiting for a long, long time to burst out of her.

'It's as if we don't matter just because we're poor and live in the workhouse. That we don't have feelings or love our families like rich people do. But we do matter and we do care. We do!'

'Of course you do,' Mrs Pankhurst said. 'Everyone does.'

'That's why women must have the vote,' Annie said. 'So we can make changes. I was sent to prison for trying to make it happen, and I'd gladly go back again, horrible as it was.'

'We can't go back to the workhouse,' Daisy said, wiping her eyes.

'And you won't,' Mrs Pankhurst promised.

Alfie tried to make himself as small as possible as Annie and Mrs Pankhurst comforted Daisy. He couldn't remember seeing her cry before, not even when they were told that the coughing fever had taken their mother.

Another boy, much older than Alfie, much older even than Daisy, came into the room in his dressing gown and slippers. He was carrying a small dog with a face a bit like a fox's.

'Hungry?' the boy asked Alfie. The little dog wagged its tail.

Alfie nodded – he was always hungry.

'Bread and jam?'

Alfie nodded even harder. They only got bread, usually stale and sometimes mouldy, with nothing on it, at the workhouse.

'This way,' the boy said.

Alfie wanted to follow him but he didn't want to leave Daisy.

'Don't worry. My mum'll look after her,' the boy said. 'She's very good at sorting out problems. My name's Harry. What's yours?'

'Alfie,' Alfie said softly.

'I bet Annie would like some bread and jam too. Prison food's pretty terrible, according to my mum and sisters. What's your sister's name?'

'Daisy.'

'I bet Daisy's hungry as well,' Harry said, and Alfie smiled at Harry and gave the little fox-faced dog a stroke. It licked Alfie's hand and Alfie wished he could have a dog of his own one day. He wondered if Sniffer had stopped barking back at the workhouse. But that made him think of Matron and he didn't want to think about her.

In the kitchen Harry took a loaf of bread from the larder and started cutting thick slices. 'I've got three big sisters called Christabel, Sylvia and Adela,' he told Alfie. 'And they all help my mum with the Women's Social and Political Union party and her Votes for Women campaign. I help too when I can. Christabel's in prison for holding up a banner saying "Votes for Women" when the MP Winston Churchill was making a speech. She loves dogs and she'd be really jealous if she knew I was looking after this one for a few days. He's a Pomeranian and his name's Brer Fox, after the Brer Rabbit stories. Do you like reading?'

Alfie nodded, although there hadn't been any books for him to read at the workhouse. The only books were the ones the teacher read to them. But at least he'd learnt to read and had gone to school for part of the time. Daisy said poor children often didn't get to go to school at all if they weren't in the workhouse.

He bit his bottom lip. 'I'm not very good at reading yet,' he admitted.

'It's just practice.' Harry grinned as he spread the thick slices of bread with lots of butter. 'You can borrow some of my books if you like. I bet you'd like the Brer Rabbit stories. And Mark Twain – he writes really exciting books.'

By the time they went back with the bread and jam Daisy had stopped crying.

While Daisy, Alfie and Annie ate hungrily, Mrs Pankhurst said that Annie, who'd been given the sack from her job while she was in prison, should join her daughter Sylvia in London as soon as possible and further the women's suffrage cause there.

'I'd like that very much!' Annie said, her eyes shining.

Mrs Pankhurst took Annie's hand and said: 'I want you to know that as long as I have a home, you must look upon it as yours, Annie. You will never have to return to factory life. Just as you two, Daisy and Alfie, will never have to return to the workhouse. Harry will take your "borrowed" clothes, clogs and blanket back to the workhouse first thing in the morning, along with a letter to the matron saying that from now on Mrs Emmeline Pankhurst, ex-Poor Law Guardian, will be employing Daisy as her maid and Alfie as her messenger boy, when he isn't at school. You may borrow some of Adela's and Harry's clothes until we get you some of your own. I think that's everything sorted out now. How does that sound?' Mrs Pankhurst asked them.

Alfie could hardly believe it. His smile stretched from ear to ear. He was so happy he thought he might never stop smiling again.

Everything had changed in one night, thanks to Mrs Pankhurst.

Brer Fox nuzzled Alfie's hand and Alfie gave him another stroke.

'Th-thank you,' Daisy said. 'We'll work hard and we won't let you down.'

'I'll be the best messenger boy ever!' Alfie told Mrs Pankhurst.

Chapter 1

The little Staffordshire bull terrier puppy's shiny black nose sniffed at the delicious smells drifting on the cold November air. The puppy was very thin and its ribs were easy to see through its white, brown and black fur.

'Jellied eels – get your jellied eels here!'

'Baked potatoes! Hot baked potatoes!'

'Oysters and whelks! Best oysters and whelks!'

'Chestnuts! Hot chestnuts!'

It was after one o'clock and lots of hungry people were buying food from the stalls and handcarts in Parliament Square Garden, across the road from the Houses of Parliament. No one was taking much notice of the thin little puppy as it trotted round the stalls.

'Meat pies!' called a vendor.

'I'll have two pies,' a man said.

As the man bit into the first pie the puppy looked up at him and gave a whine.

'Get out of it, you,' the man said, some gravy from the pie running down his chin.

A handbell clanged behind them. 'Muffins! Freshly baked muffins!'

The puppy looked longingly at the tray of muffins balanced on the baker's head. But none of the muffins fell off and the baker went on his way ringing his bell.

'Sheep's trotters – fresh sheep's trotters!' a red-faced stallholder shouted to passers-by.

The puppy drooled at the delicious meaty smell.

'Are they really fresh?' a woman asked.

'Won't find fresher,' the stallholder replied. Seizing its moment, the desperate puppy stood on its hind legs and bit into a cooked sheep's trotter from the edge of the stall.

'Hey, you! Come back here!' the stallholder shouted as the tiny dog tore off with it. 'Thief, thief!'

'I'll catch him,' yelled one of the errand boys who was hanging around the stalls hoping for work.

'Penny if you do,' said the stallholder. 'But be quick.'

'I'll be quicker than him,' said a second boy.

'Penny for whoever brings it back,' the stallholder told them.

A third, fourth, fifth and sixth boy joined in the chase. Everyone wanted the penny. They sped across the grass after the puppy, who had the warm sheep's trotter clamped in its jaws.

The puppy darted in and out of the legs of people. The boys followed, weaving in and out and trying not to trip or bump into anyone. The square was full of tourists marvelling at the majestic Houses of Parliament, where the laws of the land were made.

'Hello, puppy, that looks tasty!' Police Constable Tom Smith laughed as the small piebald dog ran between his legs. He and an elderly constable called Purvis were on their way to join the police officers lining the roads around Parliament Square Garden.

'Don't worry about that now,' Constable Purvis said, as the puppy ran into a bush to devour its prize. 'You don't want to be late, not today. We've got important work to do.'

Tom nodded and they walked on. He'd barely been able to sleep last night, he'd been so excited. It was his first day on duty as a police constable and he was going to be protecting the Houses of Parliament, because there was going to be a suffragette march. The suffragettes were campaigning for women to have the right to vote, just like men, and Tom knew that they were willing to use force. A couple of years ago there'd been a mass rally in Hyde Park with over 300,000 suffrage supporters. That one had been peaceful because it had been led by the suffragists rather than the suffragettes. Suffragists wanted the same thing as the suffragettes but they went about trying to get it by peaceful campaigning. Suffragettes were more militant. They'd attacked a member of Parliament – Mr Churchill – and rang a muffin bell continually when he'd tried to make a speech. They'd smashed the windows of 10 Downing Street, where the prime minister lived, and two of them had even chained themselves to the railings outside, in protest at the government not giving them the vote.

Tom didn't know how many women would be marching today. But the papers were full of the news that the prime minister, Mr Asquith, had gone back on his word that women who owned property and were over thirty years old would be given the vote, so there might be lots of protestors. The police had to be ready. Tom was feeling a little nervous, even though he was one of many officers: the Home Secretary, Mr Winston Churchill, had asked for six thousand policemen from all over the country to come to London and protect the Palace of Westminster. Most of them were on foot, but some looked very fierce mounted on huge police horses.

They all stood to attention as the police commissioner gave them his orders: 'The job of the police is to keep everyone calm. Crowds need to be controlled or members of the public could easily be hurt if the protest gets out of control.'

'There, it's in that bush!' Tom heard an errand boy shout as he and Constable Purvis moved to their positions across the road. He watched as the group of boys charged towards the little puppy, who ran out of the bush, across the grass and away.

Alfie loved the whistles of the steam trains as they came into the station. He and Daisy had worked for Mrs Pankhurst for four years now and had been on lots of trains with her. She travelled all over the country, speaking at rallies and marches to gain support for her political party, the Women's Social and Political Union, which was fighting for women's right to vote. Two years ago, though, she'd been sentenced to prison for six weeks when she'd tried to enter the House of Commons. That was when she'd sent Alfie and Daisy to live with Herbert and Laura Goulden, her younger brother and his wife, at their house in Winchmore Hill, north London.

'It will be far safer for you there, and I don't want either of you to be in danger or face imprisonment,' Mrs Pankhurst had told them. Daisy and Alfie had said they weren't afraid but she wouldn't listen.

'Laura has been appointed the headmistress of a brand new school called Hazelwood in Palmers Green, Alfie, and I want you to go there. Education is very important if a person is to succeed in life.'

'But –' Alfie had bitten his tongue to stop himself from saying anything more. There was no point arguing with Mrs Pankhurst.

'It's already arranged and Laura is very much in need of your help in the house, Daisy, especially now with baby Joan, and will be glad of a hard-working maid.'

'Yes, Mrs Pankhurst,' Daisy had said.

Now, Alfie had almost forgotten about his time in the workhouse four years ago. He had his own small room at Mr and Mrs Goulden's house instead of sharing a dormitory with a hundred other boys. And he got to go to school – not just in the mornings, but all day.

'We've got a lot to be thankful to Mrs Pankhurst for,' Daisy said, as if she'd read his thoughts.

'Yes, we do,' Alfie agreed, as they got off the train and caught a motorized omnibus to Caxton Street, where Mrs Pankhurst had hired a hall for the suffragettes and their supporters to meet.

'Look, that's it – there's a flag in the WSPU colours,' Daisy said, pointing to a building with a grand arched door. 'Purple for dignity, white for purity and green for hope.'

But Alfie already knew it was the right place because Mrs Haverfield and her gentle dapple-grey horse, Lightning, were there.

He stroked Lightning's soft nose. Mrs Haverfield smiled at Alfie and the horse neighed softly.

'We don't want to be late,' Daisy said, and Alfie followed her inside.

Daisy headed to the kitchen to help with the refreshments. Alfie stood at the back of the hall. The meeting had already started and Mrs Pankhurst was speaking from the stage. She was dressed in a mauve dress and long matching coat, with a dark green hat trimmed with a large white ostrich feather.

'Rather than having vast crowds of women descending on Parliament to protest about the

Prime Minister going back on his word, I have decided it would be better if there were fewer of us, just three hundred or so . . .'

Alfie thought that three hundred suffragettes was still quite a lot. It was almost as many children as there were in his whole school.

'But we will be representing the hundreds of thousands of women that desperately want and need the vote,' Mrs Pankhurst added. 'Now I will hand you over to Mrs Drummond, who will be organizing us into small groups.'

Alfie watched as a short, stout lady came forward. She had a very pink face and was wearing a red military jacket with gold tasselled epaulettes and an officer's cap on her head. Over her left shoulder she had a white sash with VOTES FOR WOMEN written on it in purple. The suffragettes called her 'The General'.

Mrs Drummond started calling out names in her big booming Scottish voice. People came forward and stood to attention in front of the stage.

Last year, The General had organized a mass rally in Edinburgh, and Alfie and Daisy had watched as a thousand women marched through the city dressed in either their working clothes or as famous women from history. The General, wearing her military clothes, led the march sitting on a horse. 'I was born in Manchester, like you,' she'd told Alfie when he'd held her horse for her. 'But we moved to Scotland when I was still a wee girl and it's where my heart is.' The General had a little son called Keir, who was three. Daisy had looked after him for the day of the march. 'That's my mammy!' he'd kept shouting excitedly as he waved his purple, white and green paper flag.

A woman standing near to Alfie put her hand up. 'Excuse me, but why do we have to go in small groups to Parliament? Wouldn't it be better if we all went at once?' she asked.

'It would,' Mrs Pankhurst agreed. 'But larger numbers aren't allowed inside and are turned away. So I've decided we'll have lots of small groups arriving at the Strangers' Entrance every few minutes instead.'

When Mrs Pankhurst was ready to leave with the first group of nine people, The General spotted Alfie at the back of the hall.

'Check what's happening out there and report back, Alfie,' she told him. 'But make sure you're not caught spying.'

'Will do,' Alfie said, and he dashed out and ran along Caxton Street, then Victoria Street to Parliament Square Garden. It was almost half a mile and took him less than ten minutes, but he knew the ladies from the WSPU would be much slower. Mrs Pankhurst had some very old ladies in her group, like Miss Neligan, who was eighty years old and couldn't walk fast, let alone run.

It was freezing and Alfie's hands were very cold, but all the running had made him thirsty, so he stopped to have a drink from the water fountain built inside a little tower on the grass.

'Well, hello there.' Alfie grinned as a little Staffie puppy came racing in, panting, with its tongue hanging out.

'Thirsty?' Alfie cupped his hands to catch some water from one of the four spouts. The puppy lapped greedily from Alfie's palms. But then it suddenly froze, trembled and ran and hid behind his legs.

'You seen a thieving puppy?' a boy wearing an errand boy's cap shouted at Alfie, poking his head round one of the columns.

'No – what did it steal?' Alfie asked him.

'A whole sheep's trotter!'

'Is it your puppy?'

'No, just a stray that's been hanging around.'

'It'll be for it when we catch it,' another boy said, as they ran off.

The puppy came out from behind Alfie's legs as soon as the boys had gone.

'Hope that sheep's trotter was worth it,' Alfie said, and the puppy wagged its tail.

He was giving it a stroke when he saw Mrs Pankhurst and her group making their way slowly towards the public entrance to the Houses of Parliament.

Clopping along behind them was Mrs Haverfield on Lightning, ready to protect the suffragettes. They all knew that confrontations with the police could turn dangerous and it was best to be careful.

'Coast's clear,' Alfie told the puppy.

The puppy looked around, as if it were checking that the shouting boys who'd chased it had really gone.

They set off together across the grass past the statues of former prime ministers. Alfie didn't know what his sister Daisy was going to say when she saw the puppy, but he really, really wanted to be able to keep it. He'd longed to have a dog of his own ever since that day he'd walked Sniffer at the workhouse and then met Brer Fox.

The puppy looked up at Alfie and wagged its tail.

Chapter 2

NOVEMBER 1910

The suffragettes carried banners that read VOTES FOR WOMEN and WHERE THERE'S A BILL THERE'S A WAY. Mrs Pankhurst and her group made their way to the entrance to the Strangers' Gallery but the gates were locked and they weren't allowed to enter the Houses of Parliament.

Constable Tom Smith stood with the line of police officers that blocked Mrs Pankhurst and her group from going back.

He wasn't enjoying his first day as a policeman. He was too worried that someone was going to get seriously hurt. And he couldn't understand why so many police were needed. His ears were ringing with the shouting of the protesters and the shrill squeals of the policemen's whistles as more small groups of suffragettes tried to reach the Houses of Parliament but were forced back with violence.

Mrs Pankhurst was shouting: 'Just arrest them. Just arrest them!'

Tom remembered the words of the police commissioner: 'Mr Churchill doesn't want any arrests. We don't want women clogging up the prisons. Just kettle them in so they're tired out and go home.' But Tom could see the passion for their cause in the suffragettes' eyes. They weren't listening to the police, and even old and disabled ladies were refusing to leave until they'd been allowed to enter

Parliament and present a petition to the prime minister.

Across the busy street, Alfie saw Mrs Pankhurst outside the entrance to the Houses of Parliament with her group of suffragettes. There were lots of policemen standing in a line in front of them. He waved but she didn't wave back and Alfie quickly put his hand down. Mrs Pankhurst had often told him it was best if as few people as possible knew that he worked for her. 'Easy for an unknown boy to slip in and out of places undetected. But not so easy for a boy who is *known*,' she always said.

Big Ben struck the half hour and the puppy shrank back and trembled with fear at the clanging of the great bell.

'It's OK,' Alfie tried to reassure the little dog. 'There's nothing to be frightened of.'

'Hey – there's the sheep-trotter thief!' one of the errand boys shouted. 'Get it!'

'Don't let it get away!' others yelled.

Alfie turned to see the gang of errand boys charging across the grass. The little Staffie took one look at the boys and ran off towards the busy road between Parliament Square Garden and the Houses of Parliament, with its tail between its legs.

'No, wait – come back!' Alfie shouted, but the puppy didn't stop. It ran across the road and disappeared into the crowds of police and protesters.

Alfie lost sight of the puppy but he ran across the road after the errand boys who were chasing it, dodging a horse-drawn carriage and a motorized omnibus with an advertisement for Pears soap on the side of it. He did his best to weave in and out of the police, who were fighting with the suffragettes. The ladies were determined to get into the Houses of Parliament and the police were determined to keep them out.

'All we want to do is deliver our petition,' Alfie heard a lady say, as an elderly policeman blocked her way.

'Why don't you go home? Back where you belong!' came the policeman's reply.

The lady knocked off his helmet and he hurried to pick it up – policemen had to pay for their own helmets.

Mrs Haverfield chose this moment to ride Lightning into the police line that was blocking Mrs Pankhurst and her group, and one of them managed to escape.

Another policeman caught the lady who'd knocked off his colleague's helmet and bent her arm behind her back.

'Stop resisting and place your other arm behind your back,' he told her as he put handcuffs on her.

Alfie saw Miss Billinghurst in her tricycle wheelchair just ahead. One minute she was in the wheelchair and the next moment she was on the ground.

Alfie ran to help her up. 'Are you OK?' he asked.

Miss Billinghurst was furious. 'Did you see that?' she shouted. 'A policeman pushed me out of my machine!'

Alfie and another suffragette helped her back into the seat.

'What kind of brute would push an invalid out of her chair?' Miss Billinghurst wanted to know.

'I'll take you back to Caxton Hall, May,' the suffragette said. 'You'll be safer there.'

But Miss Billinghurst wouldn't hear of it. 'Onwards!' she commanded. 'We'll use my wheelchair as a battering ram to get through the police lines!'

The other suffragette pushed the tricycle wheelchair down the street while Miss Billinghurst pulled her crutches from the side of her wheelchair and held them out in front of her like lances.

Constable Tom didn't know why they needed so many police for three hundred women, most of them well dressed, some quite elderly, and one or two very infirm. He didn't like how some of the police were pushing and shoving the women. He ran to help an old lady who'd been knocked over, only to be roughly pushed out of the way by three other policemen, who grabbed her and forced her into a Black Maria police carriage.

Alfie was really worried about the little Staffie. 'Have you seen a puppy?' he went around asking, but no one listened. People were too busy rushing about, the police were holding on to ladies, while other ladies were trying to pull their friends away.

'We just want to get to Parliament,' they cried.

'This is a peaceful protest.'

'We announced it in the press.'

'Votes for Women!'

'Look out!' Tom shouted, and he pushed Alfie out of the way as ten mounted police officers charged into the crowd.

Suffragettes tried to grab the horses' reins to stop them from trampling on their friends but the police forced them away.

A small smartly dressed lady wearing a Votes for Women hat and holding a large WSPU flag almost knocked Alfie over. Alfie recognized her – she had been in the first group that had left Caxton Hall with Mrs Pankhurst .

'I'm so sorry,' the lady said, and then she looked worried. 'It's Alfie, isn't it? You shouldn't be here. It's too dangerous.'

'I'm looking for a puppy,' Alfie told her. 'He's frightened. He was being chased by some boys and I don't want him to get hurt.'

'I'll see if I can spot him. But be careful!' the lady said.

'He's white, brown and black,' Alfie called after her as she ran off to help a fellow suffragette who'd been thrown to the ground.

In the midst of all the mayhem was the terrified piebald Staffie, running here and there to avoid the kicking, stamping feet of all the people. Much worse was the sudden thundering of horses' hooves. The puppy froze in terror, its eyes huge as it looked up at a police horse charging straight at it.

'No!' Alfie cried, spotting the little Staffie.

The policeman was looking straight ahead and didn't see the puppy, but the horse did. She side-stepped it at the last minute, but her back hoof sent it flying into a large pile of soft droppings left by another police horse.

By the time the puppy scrambled up, and had a quick lick, its coat was more brown than piebald.

'There, there, you're all right now,' a suffragette said, wrapping the puppy in her WSPU flag and holding it against her. The puppy was trembling. The lady was so slight that it looked big in her arms but it didn't struggle to get down and she didn't seem to want to put it down.

'Constable V700,' she told the puppy, 'needs reporting for brutality against a fellow suffragette.'

The puppy looked up at her with its big brown eyes and sneezed.

*

Alfie couldn't bear to look. He was sure the puppy had been killed. What chance did it have against a charging horse?

'Alfie,' a soft voice said, and he turned to find the lady who'd bumped into him earlier standing there, her coat torn, her hat askew and her long black hair trailing from its bun. But in her arms, wrapped in one of the big WSPU flags, was the puppy.

'Oh, thank goodness,' Alfie said, as he took the puppy from her and hugged it close.

'I put the little rascal in a flag because of the . . . the . . .'

'Road apple smell?' Alfie said, recognizing the distinctive farmyard aroma of horse manure coming from the puppy.

The lady laughed. 'I've never heard it called that before!'

'Rascal's a good name for him,' Alfie said. 'It suits him. Doesn't it, Rascal?'

The puppy gave a yap.

'Yes, it does,' said the lady. 'Only, Alfie . . .'

'Yes?'

'That puppy isn't a little boy, you know. It's a little girl.'

'Oh.' Alfie grinned. 'Well, then, she's a little Rascal.' He gave the top of the puppy's mucky head a kiss.

'Run back to Caxton Hall now and tell The General what's happening here,' the lady told Alfie. 'I escaped from the police when Lightning rode into their line, but Mrs Pankhurst and the rest of her group are still being held against the railings. You have to warn the other suffragettes about the violence they'll face when they try to reach Parliament. Not that it will stop any of them from trying.'

Chapter 3

November 1910

Victoria Street was bustling with people as Alfie ran back to Caxton Hall carrying Rascal. He'd been so worried about the puppy he'd forgotten that The General had instructed him to find out what was happening outside Parliament and report back.

Rascal's head turned from side to side as there was a shout from one direction and then another. She was surprisingly heavy, even though she'd seemed light when Alfie started running. He put her down on the ground but now there were feet to avoid everywhere: men in heavy stomping boots and ladies in long dresses with heeled shoes. Rascal gave a yelp as someone accidentally trod on her paw so Alfie picked her up again and tucked her inside his coat.

In Caxton Hall The General was organizing the next group of women to leave. Alfie ran up to her and told her what was happening.

'Mounted police on horseback are stopping the suffragettes from reaching Parliament. They have Mrs Pankhurst trapped . . .'

The General nodded. 'We've faced violence before and it won't stop us now,' she said. 'Be prepared, ladies, and protect yourselves as best you can. Anyone who'd rather not be part of the protest may stay here.'

But none of the suffragettes wanted to give up. They all wanted to try to reach Parliament with their petition.

'We can't give up now,' one said.

'It's too important,' others agreed.

Alfie turned to go back out too. He wanted to help Mrs Pankhurst and the suffragettes.

'No, Alfie, you stay here now,' The General told him. 'Mrs Pankhurst would never forgive me if you got arrested. You're too important as a go-between and scout.'

Rascal poked her furry head out of Alfie's coat.

'What in the world's that?' The General exclaimed.

'A puppy,' Alfie told her. 'I'm calling her Rascal. She landed in some horse manure, that's why she's all brown. Really she's white, brown and black.' He lifted the puppy from his coat.

'Better give Rascal a wash straight away, Alfie,' The General told him. 'Use the gentlemen's lavatory – it won't be busy today.'

Luckily Rascal was small enough to fit in one of the white porcelain sinks in the gentlemen's toilets. While Alfie was filling it with lukewarm water Rascal explored the strange room full of interesting new smells. When Alfie picked her up, she gave his face a lick. But she wasn't too sure about going in the sink full of water. She gave a squeak of protest and tried to wriggle out of Alfie's arms when he lowered her towards it.

'It's OK,' Alfie said. 'It's all right.'

He tried to dip Rascal's hind paws into the warm water but she immediately drew her legs up. She looked up at Alfie with her head tilted back, but all she could really see was his chin, so she gave that a lick. Then she let her paws touch the water and looked down at it.

'That's it, see, it's nice,' Alfie said, as he lowered her into the sink.

Rascal lapped at the water with her little pink tongue. She was very thirsty.

'Don't drink it all!' Alfie laughed as he turned on the cold tap.

Rascal thought the water gushing from the tap was even better than what was already in the sink and she started to drink that instead.

Alfie picked up the bar of coal tar soap.

'Mmm,' he said, as he sniffed at it.

Rascal tried to give the soap a lick but Alfie moved it quickly out of her reach.

'It's for washing – not eating!'

Rascal wagged her tail in the water, then looked round in surprise when it splashed her. She sat down, looked at her swishing tail and back up at Alfie as if to say, am I making those splashes?

Alfie laughed and laughed as he lathered up the coal tar soap and rubbed the suds over Rascal's fur.

'Soon have you all nice and clean again, and smelling a lot better too!' he said.

Alfie wished his friend Harry Pankhurst could have met Rascal.

'Harry would have loved you,' Alfie told Rascal. 'And he wouldn't have minded a bit what you rolled in! In fact he'd have probably just laughed.'

But Harry wasn't around to meet Rascal any more. When Alfie and Daisy had gone to live with Mr and Mrs Goulden, Harry had gone to work on a farm in Essex. Only he'd got very sick in January and Mrs Pankhurst had only just made it home from America before Harry passed away at Nurse Pine's nursing home in Notting Hill.

Alfie missed Harry very much, especially his laugh, which always made Alfie laugh too. He'd been his best friend and there'd never be anyone else like him.

While Alfie was distracted thinking about Harry, Rascal had a quick lick of the soap suds, but they didn't taste nice.

Once she was all clean, Alfie rinsed off the soap with lots of cool water and then he dried her on one of the hand towels. She liked being dried very much, even more than being washed, especially under her chin.

When she was dry and Alfie had sprayed the air around her with the lemony-smelling cologne he found in a bottle next to the mirrors, they were ready for Rascal to be seen.

'I'd say you're pretty irresistible!' Alfie told the puppy.

The hall was full of ladies and a few men who were back from their unsuccessful attempts to petition Parliament. The injured were now having their wounds seen to by Daisy and Nurse Pine.

'Oh, isn't she sweet!' one lady exclaimed.

'How utterly adorable.'

'Bring her over here so I can pet her.'

Mrs Pankhurst's younger sister, Mary Clarke, bent down to give Rascal a stroke and asked, 'Who's this little chap?' Her long hair had escaped from her bun and was swinging round her face. Rascal put out a paw to bat at it.

'She's not a chap, she's a chap-ess,' said Alfie with a grin. 'And her name's Rascal.'

'She should be our suffragette mascot.' Mary smiled. 'Would you like that?'

Rascal licked her face. She liked being stroked and made a fuss of by all the people.

'How old is she?' asked an elderly woman with a nasty cut on her head.

'I don't know,' Alfie told her. 'Not very old, I'd say.'

'Yes – just a pup.'

The only person who didn't seem entranced by Rascal was Daisy. In fact Alfie noticed her scowling at them from the other side of the room. Fortunately she was busy seeing to a lady called Ada Wright, who was loudly telling Daisy what had happened to her outside Parliament.

'The police rode at us on their shire horses, so I caught hold of the reins of one of them and wouldn't let go. A policeman grabbed my arm and twisted it until I sank to the ground. I tried to get up but was pushed over every time I did so.'

'Warrior women – fall in and line up,' The General bellowed.

'Don't go back out again, Ada,' Daisy begged. 'You've already been injured. It's too dangerous.'

But Ada wouldn't hear of it. 'We have to try and persuade the prime minister that women must have the vote,' she said as she stood up and staggered over to join the other ladies. A group of thirteen battered and bruised suffragettes had just come back from Parliament. One of them was Miss Billinghurst.

'They threw me right out of my chair,' she told The General. 'And once I'm out of it, you know I can't get back in without help. I've been paralysed from the waist down since I was a child.'

'I bet they were sorry if you raced at them in your chair, waving your crutches, like you did at the last protest,' The General said and Miss Billinghurst laughed at the memory while wincing at the pain from where she'd fallen.

Rascal was being petted by a lady who'd come back shaking with fear.

'Such a lovely little dog,' she said, tears running down her face.

'Your puppy's such a sweetie and is making everyone feel much better, Alfie. What's her name?' asked Nurse Pine, coming to attend to the shaking lady.

'Rascal,' Alfie said.

Rascal gave Nurse Pine's hand a lick and she chuckled.

'I probably taste of the arnica I've been putting on people's bruises,' she said. 'Won't do her any harm.'

'Show the government that women must be heard!' boomed The General as Ada and the others set off again for Parliament.

'You must keep your leg raised,' Daisy said to one of the women who'd just returned. Daisy lifted the woman's leg so her ankle rested on a cushion on a chair and then put a cool damp cloth on the woman's ankle.

'Thank you, dear,' the lady said.

'Arnica will help with the bruising,' Daisy added, as she gently rubbed some on to the woman's face.

'You'll make a good nurse one day, Daisy,' Nurse Pine said approvingly.

'Thank you.' Daisy smiled. 'I like to help where I can.'

'She's got a nurse's hands,' the bruised lady said.

'You know we can't keep it,' Daisy said, when she finally came over to Alfie. Rascal looked up at Daisy and wagged her tail but Daisy didn't stroke her. 'What did you bring it here for?'

'*She*,' Alfie said. 'Not "it". Her name's Rascal.'

Daisy opened her mouth but before she could say anything, the room suddenly went quiet.

All eyes were on the doorway, where Emmeline Pankhurst now stood.

Rascal immediately ran over to her, wagging her tail with delight as if the two of them had known each other for years.

'Rascal, come back,' Alfie called, running after her.

But Rascal didn't listen. She stood on her hind legs so she could stretch up to Mrs Parkhurst and wagged her tail wildly.

'Oh, how delightful,' Mrs Pankhurst said in her soft, lilting voice.

'I'm sorry, Mrs Pankhurst,' Alfie said, very embarrassed.

Mrs Pankhurst shook her head. 'Such a happy little thing and just what I needed to see on such a sad, black day. All we wanted to do was speak to the prime minister, in the name of freedom, but Mr Churchill saw to it that we were not allowed to do so.'

Rascal sat and put out her paw.

'What's his name?' Mrs Pankhurst asked Alfie.

'Rascal,' Alfie told her. 'And she's a girl puppy, not a boy.'

'I told him he couldn't keep her,' Daisy said, coming to join them. 'It's just not practical. Not without Mr and Mrs Goulden's permission.'

Alfie knew in his heart that Daisy was right: it wasn't fair to just bring Rascal home – although he was sure that Mr and Mrs Goulden would love her once they met her.

To his surprise, Mrs Pankhurst didn't agree with Daisy. As she stroked Rascal, she said thoughtfully: 'A boy with a puppy. Now what could appear more innocent than that? No one will suspect them of being spies for our cause, with secret messages to deliver, will they? I think the puppy is a splendid addition to the WSPU.'

'If you're sure Mr and Mrs Goulden won't mind,' Daisy said doubtfully.

'I am sure. Very sure,' Mrs Pankhurst told her.

It was all Alfie could do to stop himself from cheering. He scooped a surprised Rascal up in his arms as Daisy poked her tongue out at him. Rascal was going to be his puppy!

Chapter 4

November 1910

Rascal didn't take her eyes off Daisy as she added the poached eggs to a small bowl of chopped bread and mixed them together in Nurse Pine's kitchen. Two hundred suffragettes had been hurt in the confrontation with the police the day before and the most badly injured had come to stay in her nursing home in Pembridge Gardens, Notting Hill. Alfie and Daisy, as well as Mrs Pankhurst and her sister Mary, had gone there to help too.

'Go on, then!' Daisy said to Rascal when she put the bowl on the tiled floor.

Rascal gobbled up the eggs and bread in ten seconds flat.

'I bet you didn't even taste it,' scolded Daisy as Rascal gazed up with a meaningful look in her big brown eyes, head to one side, one ear up and one ear down, hoping for some more.

Alfie smiled to himself as he finished his own breakfast. Rascal certainly did have a good appetite!

Alfie liked staying at the nursing home because Nurse Pine had been so kind to Harry when Harry was sick and Mrs Pankhurst was abroad. She'd even let Alfie stay there during the Christmas holidays so Harry would have a friend with him.

'Alfie, I want you to buy a copy of all the different newspapers so I may see what the press have written about yesterday's events,'

Mrs Pankhurst said, coming in through the swing door to the kitchen.

'Yes, Mrs Pankhurst,' Alfie said, and she handed him some money.

Rascal wagged her tail as she followed him out into Pembridge Gardens. It had been very warm indoors but outside it was nice and cool. She sniffed at the interesting smells as they made their way along the quiet early-morning street.

'This way,' Alfie said, and he pushed his cold hands into his pockets.

The old newspaper seller on the corner gave Rascal a stroke and a bit of crust from his bread-and-dripping sandwich. She licked his hand to say thank you.

'Now, which paper are you after this fine crisp Saturday morning?' he asked Alfie, rubbing his hands together to try to warm them up.

'I need a copy of all of them,' Alfie said, and he hid a smile at the man's look of surprise.

'Do you indeed? Well, that is a lot of reading!'

Alfie watched the newspaper seller gather up a copy of every newspaper he had for sale.

'Thank you,' he said.

He'd just handed over the money for them when a truck juddered to a stop and a man wearing a battered bowler hat jumped out.

'I need all your copies of today's *Daily Mirror* before anyone sees them,' he said.

'That'll be a lot of ha'pennies,' the old newspaper seller said with a chuckle.

'Why are you buying them all?' Alfie asked the man, while Rascal sniffed at his boot.

'Because of the photograph on the front page. Mr Churchill thinks it could give the wrong impression of the government,' the man replied.

Rascal had had enough of sniffing his boot and put a paw out to the newspaper seller instead, hoping for more sandwich, but he was too busy collecting up all the copies of the *Daily Mirror* to notice her.

'Is that all of them?' the man asked.

'All apart from the one I just sold to this lad,' the old newspaper seller said, nodding at Alfie. 'Never had as good a morning for newspaper sales before!'

The man in the bowler hat turned to Alfie. 'Hand it over,' he demanded.

But Alfie had bought the newspaper for Mrs Pankhurst. He'd paid for it and he didn't want to give it back. He shook his head and the man looked angry.

'Give it to me – now!'

Alfie shook his head again and took a step back. The man made a grab for all the papers Alfie had under his arm, but Rascal got between them and growled and barked and jumped up, flailing her tiny paws.

'Get off, you stupid mutt!'

Alfie turned and ran off down the street and Rascal followed, hot on his heels.

'Come back here!' the man yelled.

Alfie heard the truck's noisy motor starting up and he dashed down the steps to the basement of a house, with Rascal scampering behind. Peeping out from behind the railing, they watched as the truck drove slowly and noisily down the road, stopping now and then as the driver looked for them.

Once Alfie couldn't see or hear the truck any more, he and Rascal ran up the steps and raced all the way back to the nursing home.

'Well, that was certainly quick!' Emmeline broke into a smile as Alfie and Rascal burst into the drawing room, where she and Mary were having a cup of tea.

Both Alfie and Rascal were panting hard.

'Hello, Rascal,' Mary said, patting her slender knee, and Rascal ran over to her.

Mary poured some of her tea into the saucer and Rascal lapped it up while Alfie told Mrs Pankhurst what had happened.

'Which newspaper was it that the man was told to buy?' she asked him, staring at the pile of papers Alfie had put on the small coffee table.

'The *Daily Mirror*.'

Rascal thought the tassels on the rug looked very interesting and started to tug at them with her sharp puppy teeth.

'No, Rascal!' Alfie said, stopping her just in time. 'Rugs are not for chewing.'

Rascal gave his hand a lick as Mrs Pankhurst sorted through the papers and then gave a gasp.

Alfie and Mary leant forward to see.

'Oh, my goodness,' Mary said, as they all stared at the photograph on the front page of the *Daily Mirror*. It showed a suffragette lying curled up on the road during the previous day's fray. She was trying to protect her face while a policeman loomed over her and another man tried to protect her.

'Do you know who it is?' Mary asked. 'I can't tell because she's covering her face.'

'It could be Ada Wright, judging by her build,' Emmeline said. 'But the man next to her looks like Ernestine Mills's husband, so it must be Ernestine.'

'Looking at it you can almost feel the violence and terror of the day,' Mary said.

Mrs Pankhurst agreed. 'This picture is worth more than a thousand words. Thank you for getting the paper, Alfie, and I'm sorry for the danger you and Rascal found yourselves in.'

'That's OK,' Alfie said. He was going to say he didn't mind danger, but Mrs Pankhurst was already scanning the rest of the papers to see what they had to say. Most of them had reported the terrible day as nothing more than a scuffle where a few women fainted.

' "The arrival of the Home Secretary created a stir, but Mr Churchill strode calmly through the gates as Big Ben struck twelve," ' Mrs Pankhurst read aloud.

'Huh!' said Mary.

' "One unlucky woman was accidentally hit by a car." '

'Unlucky! More like deliberately struck,' said Mary.

' "The marches on Parliament went on for six hours before the battered and bedraggled survivors finally went back to Caxton Hall." '

The two sisters looked at each other.

'Thank goodness the *Daily Mirror* is showing it for the horrendous and violent event it truly was,' Mary said.

'No wonder the government doesn't want this photograph to be seen,' Mrs Pankhurst added.

More than a hundred suffragettes had been arrested the day before and were due in court that day. One of them was Mary, who was looking very pale. Alfie wasn't sure if she was ill or if it was the worry of going to court and maybe being sent to prison. When Mrs Pankhurst had been sentenced to prison in 1908, she had been held in solitary confinement, which she'd found terribly hard.

Mrs Pankhurst took her sister's hand.

'It'll be all right,' she said. 'I'll be with you in court. You're strong and you'll survive, whatever happens.'

'I'd gladly suffer anything for the sake of freedom,' Mary said. 'I know our cause is right.'

Rascal had curled up and gone to sleep on one of the newspapers that Mrs Pankhurst had dropped on the floor.

'Alfie, I want you to show this photograph to as many of these women as you can,' Mrs Pankhurst said, writing urgently on a piece of paper. 'They'll let the others know that their suffering yesterday and possible imprisonment today wasn't in vain. We need the press on our side more than ever, so everyone can truly see what's going on and how we're being treated.'

She handed Alfie the piece of paper.

The first name on the list was Flora Drummond – The General.

'You'll find her organizing the cycling suffragettes over at Sloane Square. Miss

Billinghurst will probably be there too. Every Saturday morning they head out into the countryside to campaign and recruit more members,' Mrs Pankhurst told him.

She put the precious newspaper with its front-page photograph inside two pieces of cardboard and Alfie tucked it inside his coat.

Daisy laughed when she came in to collect the teacups and saw Alfie stuffing cardboard inside his coat. But she understood how important it was to take good care of the newspaper once she'd heard what had happened.

'There might not be many copies left if Mr Churchill's orders are obeyed and all of them get destroyed,' she said.

'Cardboard makes good armour,' Alfie told her.

Daisy nodded. 'The suffragettes could have used some cardboard armour yesterday. I've used up bottles and bottles of arnica on all their bruises.'

'Metal armour would have been even better,' Alfie said. 'Although not so easy to move about in.'

'It's better for everyone if our supporters are simply arrested rather than being hurt,' Mrs Pankhurst said.

'The women didn't stand a chance. How could anyone expect them to fight?' Alfie asked.

'And yet I have seen women fighting,' Mrs Pankhurst told him. 'One woman, in particular, who could take on a man twice her size, and throw him over her shoulder before he was even aware of what was about to happen.'

'I'd like to have seen that,' Daisy said with a grin.

'Yes, indeed,' Mrs Pankhurst said, looking thoughtful. 'More training in the art of self-defence is just what we need. Off you go with that precious newspaper now, Alfie.'

'Come on, Rascal,' Alfie said, and off they went.

Chapter 5

NOVEMBER 1910

Rascal danced round in little circles of excitement as they went through the huge wrought-iron gates of Hyde Park and then she ran off to sniff at the nearest tree.

The last time Alfie had been to Hyde Park was in the summer holidays, when he'd helped at one of the many Votes for Women rallies and marches. On that hot day, forty thousand people had gathered in the park to hear Mrs Pankhurst and the leaders of the different groups arguing for voting rights. It wasn't just women who wanted the vote. Most men couldn't vote either and wanted suffrage too. To have the right to vote you had to be over twenty-one and own your own property or pay rent of over ten pounds a year. 'It shouldn't just be rich and middle-class men who can vote,' a miner from South Wales had told the crowd. 'Everyone should have the right!' And Alfie and the rest of the men and women had cheered.

Rascal chased after a squirrel that ran up a tree and looked down at her from the top branches. It was joined by a second squirrel and Alfie was sure that, if squirrels could laugh, they'd be laughing at poor Rascal down on the grass looking up at them with her tongue hanging out.

'They won't come down until we've gone,' he told Rascal, and pressed on. After one last look at the squirrels, she ran after him.

There were only a few other dogs to sniff at in the park because it was still early, but Rascal thought the swans were interesting – until one of them hissed at her and she dashed back to Alfie. The geese flapped their wings and sped into the water, honking and squawking, when she tried to say hello to them, and the flock of pigeons pecking at some crusts of bread rose as one before she could reach them.

Rascal quickly gobbled down some of the bread before Alfie called to her: 'Come on, you've only just had breakfast! Rascal!'

Rascal wolfed down one, two, three more bits of bread – and then she came running.

Alfie wanted to walk quickly through the park but Rascal wanted to play.

She suddenly disappeared into a bush and came out with a ball in her mouth and wagged her tail at Alfie.

'Good find!' he said. He threw the ball and Rascal sped after it, picked it up in her jaws, ran back to Alfie and dropped it at his feet. She looked up at him, her brown eyes clearly saying she'd like the ball thrown again, please.

Alfie threw the ball all the way across the park until they came to the gate at the end of Serpentine Walk.

'Not far to Sloane Square now,' Alfie told Rascal as they headed down Sloane Street.

As they got closer, it was easy to spot the cycling suffragettes wearing the purple, white and green colours of the Women's Social and Political Union.

Many of the thirty or so women were wearing WSPU sashes and others held WSPU bags. Most of them had VOTES FOR WOMEN written on their hats. There was lots of laughing as they got ready for their excursion and The General had the loudest laugh of all as she strode about in her officer's peaked cap and military jacket, organizing everyone.

Rascal raced up to her with her tail wagging.

'Well, hello there,' The General said. 'What a sweet-smelling wee doggie you are now! Fine-looking puppy, Alfie. What's her name again?'

'Rascal,' he said.

'And I bet she is a little rascal!' The General laughed as Rascal wagged her tail, and Alfie laughed too.

Rascal made her way round the other suffragettes so she could be stroked by them as well.

Mrs Pankhurst had told Alfie how she and her family used to be keen cyclists. 'Being on a bicycle gives a woman a sense of freedom and adventure,' she'd said with a smile.

All of the suffragettes' bicycles were decorated with purple, white and green rosettes, ribbons and flags.

'Mrs Pankhurst wanted you to see this,' Alfie said to The General, pulling the newspaper from his coat.

Everyone gathered round to look at the front page.

When Miss Billinghurst arrived in her tricycle wheelchair, Rascal hopped up into her lap.

'Sorry about that!' Alfie said, running to grab Rascal.

'Oh, that's all right,' Miss Billinghurst said. 'I just wish we could take her with us on our jaunt out to West Wickham to recruit more members for the WSPU. The more women we can get pushing Parliament to give us the vote the better!'

'Rascal needs to go with Alfie. They've got a very important job to do,' The General said, showing her the picture of the suffragette lying on the ground. 'The government's trying to get hold of all the copies of the paper to stop people from seeing what really happened yesterday.'

'Who's next on your list, Alfie?' Miss Billinghurst asked.

Alfie gulped when he saw the next name.

'"Princess Sophia Duleep Singh, Faraday House, Hampton Court",' he read aloud. Would he really be permitted to meet a princess?

'Hampton Court!' The General tutted loudly. 'It'll take you all day to walk there from here.' And she strode over to the railings where the decorated bikes were resting.

'The princess lives in a house Queen Victoria gave her,' Miss Billinghurst told Alfie, as she gave Rascal, still on her lap, a stroke. 'It's called Faraday House, after Professor Faraday, who invented electricity, and it's on the road opposite Hampton Court Green.'

Still worried about meeting a princess, Alfie bit his bottom lip and watched The General taking the suffragette ribbons and rosettes off one of the bicycles.

Rascal wagged her tail and jumped off Miss Billinghurst's lap to catch one of the trailing ribbons.

'Oh, go on then, wee doggie, you can play with it,' The General said.

Rascal gave the ribbon in her mouth a good shake while making happy puppy growling sounds.

'Better use this,' The General said, bringing the bike over to Alfie. 'Faraday House isn't hard to find on a bicycle. You just cycle through Richmond Park, then Bushy Park and you can't miss it when you reach Hampton Court Green.'

Alfie looked down at the bike and then back up at The General.

'For me?' he said, unable to quite believe it. He'd never had his own bicycle before, although Harry had taught him to ride his.

'You'll get to Hampton Court in less than half the time,' The General said. 'Should take you about an hour if you don't dilly-dally. And keep hold of it when you're done today. You never know when you might need it for other missions.'

Alfie grinned and lifted Rascal into the fish basket on the back.

'See you soon, Alfie,' the suffragettes said as they too got on their bicycles.

'See you soon!' Alfie called back, smiling at The General. 'And thank you.'

'You're most welcome, Alfie,' she said.

'That's it, you stay in your basket,' Alfie told Rascal. He pushed down on the pedals, which he could only just reach, and they sped towards Hampton Court, with Rascal lifting her head to feel the breeze rushing through her fur.

Chapter 6

November 1910

Alfie had never been to Hampton Court Palace before, but he had heard of it. Mrs Goulden loved history and she'd told his class at Hazelwood School all about how the magnificent palace had been built for Cardinal Wolsey, but King Henry VIII had taken it from him and kept it for himself.

As Alfie cycled through Richmond Park, Rascal stood up in her basket to look at the red deer but fortunately didn't jump out. They didn't see any more deer until they went through Bushy Park, and this time Rascal was brave enough to give a high yap. The deer looked over at her, gave a flick of their short tails and then went back to eating grass.

Alfie grinned to himself, sure that the puppy would have run off terrified if the deer had headed towards them.

They'd been cycling for just over an hour when Alfie caught his first glimpse of the magnificent palace. Because the bicycle The General had given him was a bit too big, he wobbled as he came to a halt and only just managed to get one foot on the ground to stop it from toppling over. Rascal made a little sound of fear at the sudden unsteadiness of her basket.

Alfie stared up at the huge and imposing red brick palace. He counted twenty square windows along the top, twenty round ones beneath them, then forty rectangular ones divided into two rows below those, and that was just the part of the palace that was facing him.

A boy with three small dogs and two big ones appeared in the distance. Alfie thought the boy looked about the same age as him so he raised a hand to wave and the boy waved back. As soon as Rascal saw the boy and the dogs, she gave a yap of delight, jumped out of the bicycle basket and went haring across the grass towards them.

'Rascal, come back!' Alfie shouted.

But Rascal was too excited to listen and she didn't return. Alfie laid the bike on the grass and ran after her.

'I'm Manna Singh,' the boy said when Alfie reached him. 'Who are you, and what is your puppy's name?'

'I'm Alfie,' Alfie told him. 'And my puppy's called Rascal.'

'Because she can be a rascal?' the boy asked.

'Yes!' Alfie laughed and Manna laughed too.

'She's just a puppy,' Manna said.

Alfie nodded. 'I'm here to show something to Princess Sophia Duleep Singh,' he said. He was still more than a bit worried about meeting a princess and not sure if he was supposed to call her your majesty, or princess, or what exactly. 'Do you know which of these houses is Faraday House?' he asked, pointing at the grand houses across the road opposite the green.

Manna grinned.

'What is it?' Alfie asked.

'My father is Princess Sophia Duleep Singh's kennel master and the dogs Rascal is so happily playing with are the princess's prized Pomeranians and Borzois. The princess's great-grandfather was a kennel master called Manna too – or at least he was a kennel master until his daughter, Jindan, married Maharajah Ranjit Singh, the great king of the Sikh empire. I'm named after Manna and so is my dad.'

'I'm named after my dad as well,' Alfie said. 'Although I never met him.'

He often wondered what his father had been like. But when he'd asked Daisy about him, all she could really remember was him singing her a lullaby when she was little.

'So which one is the princess's house?' Alfie asked.

'That one with the pink flowers growing up it,' Manna said, pointing to a three-storied house. 'But she isn't there now. My dad drove her to London to appear at Bow Street Magistrates' Court along with the other suffragettes who were arrested yesterday.'

As Manna was speaking, a shiny black car pulled up and the princess's dogs, followed by Rascal, started racing across the grass towards it. A small lady bundled up in a fur coat, wearing a hat with purple feathers, got out of the car.

'That's her – that's the princess!' Manna said, and he started running after the dogs, with Alfie right behind him.

'Hello, Alfie,' the woman said in a soft voice when they reached her. Alfie recognized her as the lady who'd helped to rescue Rascal from the horses' hooves outside the Houses of Parliament the day before.

'Your Highness,' said Manna, giving a small bow.

'Oh – oh,' said Alfie, suddenly not able to speak. 'I didn't know it was you . . . I'm sorry . . . your Highness.'

The princess gave Rascal a stroke. 'And how are you, dear little Rascal?' she asked the puppy.

'A lot cleaner than the last time you saw her.' Alfie laughed and then got embarrassed again because he was talking to a real-life princess.

To his surprise, the princess chuckled softly.

'No road apples today,' she said.

Rascal rubbed her face against the princess's soft coat.

'She is such a lovely, friendly little pup.'

The princess's warm smile made Alfie feel brave enough to ask her about her trip to court. 'What happened at the trial this morning?' he ventured.

'Winston Churchill ordered that all the charges against the suffragettes who were arrested yesterday be dropped, but I'm still going to write and complain about the police violence,' she said. 'Someone could have been killed.'

Rascal wagged her tail to agree but the next moment she was pushed out of the way by one of the Pomeranians.

'And you're lovely too,' Princess Sophia said to it. 'And you and you,' she added, giving each of the dogs a stroke in turn.

'Mrs Pankhurst wanted you to see this picture in the *Daily Mirror* showing the truth about what happened yesterday – if you haven't seen it already,' Alfie said, pulling the newspaper from inside his coat.

Princess Sophia gave a gasp as she looked at the picture.

'That poor woman! I can almost feel her terror.'

Rascal nudged the princess's hand with her head and Princess Sophia petted her.

'But I'm very glad you were found on that day, Rascal, and were unharmed. Very glad indeed,' she said. 'Who's next on your list to see the paper, Alfie?'

'Mrs Pankhurst's daughter Sylvia in the East End, then to the West End to show her other daughter, Christabel, at the WSPU headquarters, then Ada Wright at Westminster Mansions, Ernestine Mills, Evelina Haverfield at Yorke Street, Mrs Fawcett, and finally Mrs Brackenbury and her daughters at Campden Hill Square, before I head back to Nurse Pine's nursing home,' Alfie told her. 'We're going home to Mr and Mrs Goulden's house tomorrow. I just hope they won't mind having Rascal living with them too.'

'I'm sure they won't,' Princess Sophia reassured him, as she opened her handbag and took out her purse.

Alfie wasn't so sure. Maybe Daisy was right – but he didn't want her to be. At least Mrs Pankhurst had given her approval.

'I want to send you back with a donation for the WSPU,' the princess said, and she handed Alfie a five-pound note, and then added a penny to it.

'Make sure you give Mrs Pankhurst the penny too. Donations ending in a one are said to be lucky in India.'

Alfie promised he would and the princess gave him two more pennies.

'One for you, and one for you to spend on dear little Rascal.'

'Thank you, your Highness,' Alfie said.

'I will write to you and hope to see you again very soon,' Manna said, as Alfie gave each of the princess's dogs a stroke and Rascal wagged her tail goodbye.

By the time Alfie had shown the paper to everyone on Mrs Pankhurst's list, it was after seven o'clock at night. Rascal had fallen asleep in her bicycle basket as Alfie cycled up to the nursing home. She was so tired that Alfie had to carry her inside, but she immediately woke up at the delicious smell of the chicken and vegetable stew Daisy had waiting for them.

Chapter 7

December 1910

Every morning Rascal raced to the front door of Mr and Mrs Goulden's house as soon as she heard the gate open and boots walking up the garden path.

'Morning, Rascal!' the postman called out from the other side of the door.

Rascal had first met the postman on the morning after she'd arrived with Alfie and ever since then had made a point of greeting the strange man who put paper things through the hole in the door but didn't knock or come in.

Now she stood up on her back legs and wagged her tail as the letters landed with a soft plop on the doormat.

Usually Alfie picked the letters up before she could get to them.

'No toothmarks or slobber on them, thank you,' he'd say.

But today he was still in the kitchen. Rascal scratched at the letters with her paws and managed to pick one up in her mouth. She trotted to the kitchen with it, very proud of herself.

Alfie's mouth fell open when he saw her.

'What have you got there?'

Rascal dropped the letter on the floor. Then sat down and looked up at Alfie with her head to one side.

'Good puppy!' Alfie said, and he gave her a stroke and the corner of his toast and marmalade. 'It's from Manna,' he told Daisy, who was making more toast, as he tore the envelope open. It was the third letter Manna had written to him in the past five weeks.

My dear friend Alfie,
    I hope you and Rascal are well and enjoying the icy weather. (I am not.) My father says there are places in India where you can find snow but I prefer the sun! I hope you get many wonderful presents for Christmas and that I see you in the New Year.
    Your friend,
    Manna Singh

Alfie immediately wrote back:

Dear Mamma,

Merry Christmas and New Year to you too.

Rascal and I are very well. She has a new basket in the kitchen that Mr Goulden bought for her and she loves to curl up in it.

Next year has a one at the end of it – so I expect it will be a very lucky year!

Alfie chewed the end of his pencil as he remembered how worried he'd been that Mr and Mrs Goulden wouldn't like Rascal. But it had turned out that they didn't just like her – they loved her, and so did their three-year-old daughter, Joan. Rascal loved them too, and their big garden, and next door's friendly ginger cat, who came to visit sometimes.

The doorbell rang and Rascal trotted after Daisy as she went to answer it. Two men stood outside with a small tree that smelt unlike any other tree Rascal had smelt. She sniffed and sneezed at the pine smell.

'Where would you like it?' one of the men asked Daisy.

'In the drawing room,' Daisy told them.

'Righty-ho,' the man said.

Rascal scampered along beside them, wagging her tail, before running to the kitchen to find Alfie.

'Alfie, can you help decorate the Christmas tree?' Daisy called from the drawing room.

Alfie hurried to help, with Rascal almost dancing along behind him. The rest of his letter to Manna would have to wait until later.

Rascal caught the smell of mice coming from the box of Christmas decorations on the floor. She put her nose into the box as soon as it was opened. But the mouse family had long gone, and there were only glass baubles and angels left.

'Out of the way, Rascal,' Alfie said.

Rascal sneezed again at the pine smell and watched as Daisy and Alfie carefully placed the decorations on the Christmas tree.

'Holly next,' Daisy said.

Next door's cat watched from the fence as they cut holly from the garden to decorate the drawing room.

Rascal came out with her ball but Alfie was too busy to play.

'Not now, Rascal,' he said, hurrying back inside with his arms full of holly branches.

Rascal ran to the front door to greet Mrs Pankhurst and her sister Mary when they arrived late in the afternoon. Mary had only recently been let out of Holloway prison and

Alfie thought she looked very pale and tired when he opened the door

'Emmeline and Mary,' Mr Goulden said, as he kissed his two older sisters on the cheek. 'It's so good to have you here for Christmas.'

'Come on into the warm,' Mrs Goulden said, as Rascal, very excited, danced around them all.

'Sylvia was so entranced by little Rascal when she met her that she made her this,' Mrs Pankhurst said, pulling a purple, white and green dog collar and matching lead from her handbag and giving them to Alfie.

Rascal rubbed her face against Mary's long coat and looked up at her.

'You know, Rascal really looks as if she's smiling sometimes,' Mary said.

'I know,' laughed Alfie, looking down at Rascal's sweet funny little face.

Alfie was smiling and Mrs Pankhurst and Mary were stroking her, so Rascal felt she must have done something good, even though she wasn't sure what.

'And sometimes if Rascal wants something really badly, like me to play ball with her, she'll give me a big cheeky grin!' Alfie added.

At the sound of the word 'ball', Rascal looked over at the door that led to the kitchen, where she kept her ball in her basket, and then back up at Alfie. Were they going for a walk?

'Seeing her funny smiling face makes my heart sing,' Mary said.

Rascal was very excited when Daisy brought in tea and sandwiches and ginger cake. The last time she'd met Mary, she'd given her a saucer of tea. Rascal watched Mary closely as she drank her first cup, willing her to give her some.

'Oh, Rascal, poor Mary hasn't had a decent cup of tea for the past month while she's been in prison, and now you want to share it with her!' Mrs Pankhurst scolded as Mary poured some of her tea into the saucer and gave it to the puppy.

Rascal lapped it all up and then looked directly at Mary and wagged her tail.

'Prison would have been a lot easier if I could have had you there with me,' Mary told Rascal as she gave her a stroke. 'You would have made the other suffragettes suffering there laugh too.'

'We have to keep fighting until every little girl born has the same rights as her brothers,' Mrs Pankhurst said, squeezing her sister's hand.

'Yes, we do,' agreed Mr Goulden, coming into the drawing room carrying little Joan.

'Whatever the cost,' agreed his wife, Laura, behind him. Joan stretched out her hand to Rascal, who she loved to play with.

Mary nodded as she slowly sipped her second cup of tea, with Rascal watching her.

Mr and Mrs Goulden were strong supporters of Votes for Women and held meetings at Hazelwood School in the evenings. Alfie and Daisy helped by looking after little Joan, making tea and serving sandwiches and cakes, taking hats and coats and showing people to their seats.

It didn't seem fair to Alfie that some people were allowed to vote and others weren't. But then he thought a lot of things weren't fair – like being sent to the workhouse because his mum couldn't afford to pay the rent after his dad died.

There was usually a reporter and often a photographer from one of the newspapers at the Hazelwood School meetings, as well as the police. Sometimes the meetings turned rowdy and people started singing or shouting to drown out the speakers, and a few times eggs and flour had been thrown. Alfie had been glad the police were there then, even if it did feel like they were spying on the suffragettes.

Rascal woke up on Christmas Day to a kitchen full of the most delicious meaty smell coming from the oven. It was so good that she went and sat next to the oven, drooling.

'Rascal, you're getting in the way,' Daisy told her.

Rascal moved away for a little while but then went to sit next to it again.

Late in the morning she was given her first taste of turkey.

'Not too much, now,' Alfie said. 'Too much isn't good for your tummy.'

Rascal looked down at her empty bowl and then up at Alfie and gave a whine.

'Walkies?' Alfie said, and he opened his hand to reveal the new red ball that he'd bought for her with the money from Princess Sophia. Rascal looked at the ball and then at Alfie as if to say, is it really for me?

'Yes, it's for you. It's your Christmas present,' Alfie said.

Rascal looked at the ball again and wagged her tail.

'Let's go,' said Alfie, and Rascal trotted after him wearing the new collar that Sylvia Pankhurst had made for her.

At nearby Grovelands Park, Alfie threw the ball for Rascal and she chased it across the grass. There were no other dogs in the park for her to play with today and the ducks had all disappeared on to the island in the centre of the boating lake.

Rascal put her tongue out to taste the white flakes that started to float down from the sky. Soon she was racing around, biting and snapping at them.

'You'll never catch them all!' Alfie laughed as he watched his funny little pup. He was so glad he had found her. So very glad. This was the best Christmas ever.

'Rascal!' Alfie called, holding his arms out. Rascal dashed over to him and dropped her ball at his feet. 'One more throw,' Alfie said.

After *ten* more throws, they ran back to the house. The kitchen was toasty and warm after the cold park.

'*Brrrr*,' Alfie said, hanging his coat on the back of a chair.

Rascal dropped her new ball next to her old one and then curled up in her basket.

Daisy came into the kitchen, her eyes red.

'What's happened?' Alfie asked her.

'Mrs Clarke's been taken ill,' she told him. 'The doctor's with her now. Alfie – it's serious.'

She filled a bowl with hot water and headed back to the drawing room as Alfie stared after her. Rascal whined.

They stayed in the kitchen out of the way and it wasn't until the next morning that Alfie found out Mary had died.

'She was such a lovely lady,' Daisy said, blowing her nose. 'So caring.'

Alfie nodded. 'Rascal loved her.'

He looked round. Where was the puppy?

'Have you seen Rascal?' he asked Daisy.

Daisy shook her head.

Rascal's basket was empty. But her ball was still there.

Alfie hoped she hadn't gone upstairs to the bedrooms, which she was strictly forbidden to do. He went to check, but as he hurried past the drawing room he saw Rascal was in there with Mrs Pankhurst. The puppy was sitting close to her feet and Mrs Pankhurst was dabbing at her eyes with a handkerchief.

Alfie tried to slip away unseen but Rascal spotted him in the doorway and wagged her tail. Mrs Pankhurst looked up and beckoned Alfie in. Her eyes were red from crying.

'She's gone, Alfie,' she said. 'My darling, sweet sister Mary has gone. I don't know how I shall bear it – 1910 started off such a terrible year with dear Harry's death, and now it has ended horribly with Mary's. All I hope is that the two of them are together in heaven.'

Mary had been in charge of the suffragettes in Brighton and lots of her friends came to Southgate for the funeral. Alfie wasn't going to take Rascal to the cemetery for the funeral but Mrs Pankhurst said he should.

'Mary loved her so and would have liked her to be there,' she said.

Alfie and Rascal looked at the wreaths outside the church while the service took place inside. On one of the wreaths were the words I GLADLY PAY FOR THE PRICE OF FREEDOM.

'It was what she said when she received her last prison sentence,' Mrs Pankhurst told Alfie when the service was over. 'I won't let her death be in vain. "Deeds not Words": that's what we need now more than ever.'

Chapter 8

Spring 1911–March 1912

Rascal dashed past Mr Goulden to the front door, wagging her tail. But it wasn't her friend the postman, who sometimes gave her a bit of biscuit from his pocket. When Mr Goulden opened it, there was a man holding a large briefcase, looking glum in the spring sunshine.

'May I help you?' Mr Goulden asked him.

'I'm here to deliver the census forms,' the man said.

'Oh, yes.' Mr Goulden invited the man in and asked Daisy to make him a cup of tea.

In the drawing room Rascal sat next to the man and looked pointedly at him, but he didn't pour any of his tea into the saucer for her.

'Thirty-six thousand of us have been hired to distribute the 1911 census forms and collect them in on the third of April,' the man told Mr Goulden as he slurped his tea. 'It'll record where everyone slept on the night of the second of April: the residents of the house, their age and their employment.'

Rascal put her paw out to the man but he drank the last few drops of tea and then put the cup down on the saucer, empty. Rascal made a sad little sound and lay down with her head on her paws.

'We'll see you on the third of April, then, with the form all filled in ready for you,'

Mr Goulden said, as he and Rascal showed the man to the door.

'That you will,' said the man.

On 2 April Rascal was very busy running back and forth to the front door to greet the twenty ladies that arrived during the day.

'Welcome, welcome,' Mr Goulden said, as he ushered them in.

Rascal loved all the fuss she was given, especially when some of the women threw her ball for her in the garden.

In the kitchen Alfie helped Daisy make sandwiches and drinks for everyone.

'What are they all doing here?' he asked his sister. There were suffragettes everywhere.

'They're hiding here overnight, so they can't be counted in this year's census,' Daisy told him. 'It's to protest about women not being given the vote.'

'But where will everyone sleep?' Alfie asked Daisy. There weren't enough beds or even chairs for everyone.

'I doubt there'll be much sleeping going on here tonight!' Daisy laughed.

And she was right. Everyone was in very high spirits – they sang round the piano and played cards and charades until well after midnight. Rascal got so tired she went to sleep under the table.

'If the government won't let us vote, although it still expects us to pay taxes, then we won't let ourselves be counted in the census,' the women said.

'Women don't count, so we won't be counted!'

'But won't you get into a lot of trouble?' Alfie asked them.

'A five-pound fine or a month in prison,' one lady said.

Alfie thought that was indeed a lot of trouble for not filling in a form.

'Mrs Pankhurst is over in Aldwych, hiding at an ice-skating rink with lots of other suffragettes.'

Alfie had never been ice skating and he wished he could have gone there with Mrs Pankhurst – although Rascal might not have liked it and her paws would get frozen on the ice. An image of Rascal trying to skate came into his head and he smiled to himself.

'I heard thousands of women all over the country are going to do the same as us,' one suffragette laughed.

'Mrs Pankhurst and her daughter Christabel have been busy arranging it and sending out messages from headquarters,' said another.

Alfie took an empty sandwich plate back to the kitchen. They hadn't seen Mrs Pankhurst since Mary's funeral, and he hadn't been asked to deliver any messages for her or the WSPU either. It hadn't stopped him practising different routes on his bike, though, or cycling into central London. He and Rascal had even been as far as Hampton Court to see Manna and the princess's dogs.

Up in his room Alfie tossed and turned, but couldn't get to sleep because of the noise from downstairs, and because he was worrying that Mrs Pankhurst didn't want him to be her messenger boy any more.

Early the next morning all of the suffragettes left and when the census man came later to collect the form there was nothing written on it about the overnight visitors.

The whole of 1911 went by without Alfie seeing Mrs Pankhurst – she didn't come to the Gouldens' house, and she spent Christmas in America.

On New Year's Eve, Mr and Mrs Goulden called Daisy and Alfie into the drawing room to toast the end of 1911 and the beginning of 1912 with fruit punch. Rascal and little Joan played on the floor together.

'To absent friends and family,' Mr Goulden said, and Alfie thought about Mary and Harry, who would never come back, and Mrs Pankhurst, who he hoped would be back soon.

He stroked Rascal's furry head and she looked up at him with her big brown eyes.

A few months later Alfie was sitting at his desk at Hazelwood School one Friday afternoon when a school monitor came in and spoke to his teacher, Miss Franklin.

'Alfie, please go to the headmistress's office,' Miss Franklin said.

Alfie could feel all the other children staring at him and wondering what he'd done as he stood up and left the classroom.

'Come!' Mrs Goulden called when he tapped on her door.

Alfie was astonished to find Mrs Pankhurst sitting on a chair in Mrs Goulden's office.

'Alfred,' she said with a smile. 'My, you've grown. As has your dog. I thought Rascal might not remember me, but judging by how excited she was when I went to the house, I think she must do.'

'It's good to see you, Mrs Pankhurst,' Alfie said, feeling shy after all this time of not seeing her.

Mrs Pankhurst looked a lot older and thinner, and there were deep lines around her eyes and across her forehead.

'I want you to take this to Lizzie Holsworth over in the East End. It's very urgent,'

Mrs Pankhurst told Alfie, holding out a small packet wrapped in sacking and tied with string.

Alfie looked at the address on the label and frowned. 'Bryant and May factory,' he said.

'It's where the match girls' strike of 1888 took place,' Mrs Goulden reminded him. She had talked about the strike in assembly one day.

'That strike made a big difference to the dreadful working conditions of women at the factory,' Mrs Pankhurst said. 'And I'm proud to have been part of the strike committee and done all I could to help at the time. But working conditions are still a long way from being perfect.'

Alfie remembered what Mrs Goulden had told them: 1,400 women and girls had gone on strike at the match factory because of the long, fourteen-hour working days, poor pay, fines for being late and the deadly health risk from the white phosphorous that was used to make the matches. White phosphorous hadn't been allowed to be used since 1910 and now red phosphorous was used to make the matches.

Alfie looked down at the small parcel that Mrs Pankhurst had given him. It had something hard that was shaped like a capital T inside it.

'What is it?' he asked before he could stop himself.

'Best you don't know, my dear,' Mrs Pankhurst told him.

Alfie bit his bottom lip. He should have known better than to ask Mrs Pankhurst. She always said that if he were questioned by the police, the less he knew and was able to tell them the better.

'Get there as quickly as you can, but don't take any risks,' Mrs Pankhurst told him. 'Here's some money for expenses.' She handed him two shillings.

'You can leave school early to take the parcel,' Mrs Goulden said. 'Hurry along now.'

'I'll go home and get my bicycle,' Alfie said.

'No need. Daisy has it outside waiting for you, along with dear Rascal,' Mrs Pankhurst told him. 'Remember, it's urgent.'

Rascal was very excited to see Alfie and wagged and wagged her tail. She'd never been to his school before and usually waited most of the day by the back door at the Gouldens' house for him to come home.

'Oh, no – she doesn't have her suffragette collar on,' Alfie said. He usually put the purple, white and green collar on Rascal when they went out because she looked so smart in it.

'Best if no one knows who she is for this trip,' Daisy said, as they headed away from the school.

'I wonder what's inside this parcel that's so urgent,' Alfie said to his sister. But Daisy just shrugged.

'I made two packets of sandwiches for you and Rascal. One's chicken and the other is dripping. They're in your bicycle basket, but I wouldn't leave them there – unless you want Rascal to eat them!'

Alfie grinned. Rascal did love tasty food – or any food, even if it wasn't all that tasty.

Daisy went with them down Hazelwood Lane towards the main road but when she saw the tram she started running towards the tram stop.

'Where are you going?' Alfie called after her.

But Daisy didn't stop.

'Things to do!' she shouted as she jumped on the tram, which headed off along Green Lanes towards Wood Green.

Alfie shook his head. It wasn't like Daisy to be so secretive, but recently she'd been disappearing off in the evenings, and when he asked her where she'd been she'd told him it was best he didn't know. It was very annoying!

Rascal made herself as comfortable as possible in the basket on the back of the bike. Now that she was fully grown it was a bit small for her, but at least Daisy had put her ball in the basket too. Rascal could still smell the chicken and dripping sandwiches that Daisy had made but Alfie had put those in his coat pocket.

When Alfie had been given the bike by The General, his feet had only just reached the pedals, but now it was the perfect size for him and he was proud of how fast he could go on it.

It took a little less than an hour to reach the East End from Palmers Green. As Alfie cycled towards the factory, the buildings became more derelict and the children on the street were without shoes and wore clothes that were little more than dirty rags.

'Got anything to eat?' one of them shouted.

A group of children crowded round, holding out their hands, begging.

Alfie pulled the first packet of sandwiches his fingers touched from his coat and threw them to the children. Then he pressed down on the pedals as some of them started running after him. Alfie cycled faster, afraid they might try to take his bicycle or, worse, take Rascal.

He was relieved to cycle past the railway station and through the big wrought-iron gates of the factory, leaving the children behind. But he'd never been inside a factory before and he didn't know where he was supposed to go.

There was a gatekeeper in a little lodge next to the big red-brick factory buildings but Alfie didn't want to speak to him. Mrs Pankhurst had made it clear that the mysterious parcel had to be kept secret and must be given to Lizzie Holsworth in person. Fortunately the tea-break horn went off and a girl of about the same age as Alfie came out through the swing doors while he was wondering what to do.

'Excuse me, I'm looking for Lizzie Holsworth. Do you know where she is?' Alfie asked her.

'She'll be out the back,' the girl said. 'I'll show you.'

'Thanks.'

Rascal hopped down from the basket and gave a wag of her tail as Alfie pushed the bike down the path after the girl. There were eleven or twelve women in the small paved yard at the back.

'There's Lizzie,' said the girl, pointing.

Rascal saw Lizzie walking towards them and wagged her tail and gave a whine. Lizzie was carrying a large ball.

'Mrs Pankhurst gave me this to give to you,' Alfie told Lizzie, holding out the parcel.

Lizzie took it from him with a nod, while Rascal sat down, looked up at the ball and put out her paw.

'Here we go, girls!' Lizzie shouted.

The factory women ran to their positions as Lizzie threw the football into the middle of the yard. As soon as Rascal saw the football flying through the air, she raced towards it, barking with excitement.

Lizzie laughed. 'We used to have a dog just like yours when I was a kid. My dad said she was the gentlest dog he'd ever known.'

In no time at all, a charging, laughing game of football was in progress, with Rascal in her element in the midst of it all. It looked so much fun that Alfie joined in too.

The tallest woman Alfie had ever seen stood ready in the goal, which was marked by two aprons.

'Go on, then, let's see if you can get that ball past our Gail,' the other women said to Alfie.

Alfie had learnt to play football at school. He took a deep, steadying breath as the goalkeeper widened her stance and held out her arms.

He positioned the ball on the ground, took a few steps back and then ran at it from the right as if he were going to score with his right foot, but at the last moment he kicked it with his left foot instead. The ball shot past a surprised Gail straight into the goal.

'Good shot,' said Gail.

'Lucky shot!' shouted one of the girls. 'Bet he can't do it again.'

Rascal darted over to try and grab the ball but Gail scooped it up.

'Best of three!' she shouted to Alfie.

Alfie ran at the ball and kicked it towards the left side of the goal, but this time Gail managed to stop it.

'Good try, though,' Gail said.

Alfie grinned and kicked the ball a third time – and missed.

But Rascal didn't. She dashed forward, grabbed the ball in her mouth and ran off with it.

'Bring that ball back, Rascal!' Alfie called.

Rascal thought she'd much rather keep it, so the football match turned into a game of chase as the women and Alfie charged after Rascal, trying to get the ball back.

'Here, Rascal,' Alfie said, breaking off a piece of the sandwich he had left in his pocket.

Rascal stared at it for a few seconds, then she dropped the ball, sat down and put out her paw – definitely food before ball.

It was time they were going, but when Alfie looked round for Lizzie to say goodbye she'd disappeared. Worse, the spot where he'd left his bike was now empty.

'Have you seen my bicycle?' Alfie asked the other women as they headed back into the factory.

But no one had.

Alfie felt a sick, hollow feeling in his stomach. Someone had stolen his bicycle.

Rascal looked up at Alfie's sad face and whined.

Lying by the wall where he'd leant his bike was the sacking from Mrs Pankhurst's parcel. Alfie picked it up and a piece of paper dropped out. 'Oxford Street 6 p.m.' was written on it.

Could Lizzie have taken his bicycle? It seemed the only explanation. It was after five o'clock already. Had she taken it so she could get to Oxford Street by six?

'Come on, Rascal,' Alfie said, and they ran out of the factory gates to Bow railway station. They'd never catch a bicycle thief on foot but they might reach Oxford Street by six o'clock if they went on the train.

Alfie was determined to get his bike back. He knew where Lizzie had gone and he'd follow her!

Rascal wasn't at all sure about the noisy steam train when it came into the station. She backed away from it, but Alfie held out more of the chicken sandwich and it was too much for her to resist.

'Good dog!' Alfie said when she hopped on to the train, and he gave her the rest of the sandwich, which she gulped down in no time at all.

A moment later the floor of the carriage started rumbling. Rascal trembled with fear and then jumped into Alfie's lap when the whistle blew.

'It's OK,' Alfie said. 'I won't let anything hurt you.'

Rascal stayed on Alfie's lap until they reached the end of the line at Fenchurch Street. They then caught an omnibus, which was a lot less frightening than the train.

It was almost six o'clock and twilight by the time they got off the bus at Oxford Street and headed past the colourful window displays of

Selfridges department store. The street was busy with shoppers and people heading home from work, and Alfie didn't know how he was going to find Lizzie. Suddenly there was the sound of smashing glass and chaos broke out as women from all directions started breaking shop windows.

Alfie was worried Rascal would cut her paws on the shattered glass. He picked her up and crossed the road, but windows started to be smashed on that side of the road too.

Alfie gasped when he saw Lizzie from the match factory standing next to a broken window.

'Lizzie!' he shouted.

She looked round, saw him and then ran off.

Alfie and Rascal ran after her but soon lost her in the crowds. People were shouting and pointing, and police whistles were blowing. Just ahead of them, Alfie spotted Miss Billinghurst in her tricycle wheelchair.

'Here you go, girls!' she called as she passed a group of women, pulling something small and shiny from under the blanket covering her legs. She tried to hand it to the women but it slipped from her fingers and fell to the ground. Without thinking, Alfie ran over to pick it up. It was a tiny silver toffee hammer. So that was what the suffragettes were using to break all those windows! Just as Alfie was handing the hammer back to Miss Billinghurst, he looked up to see a policeman pointing at him.

'*Vandal!*'

The policeman blew his whistle and charged towards Alfie and Rascal as another policeman grabbed hold of Miss Billinghurst's wrists and arrested her.

For a second Alfie froze. He hadn't hit any windows, he hadn't smashed anything. But would the policeman believe that when he was holding a hammer? Alfie didn't think so.

From the darkness a hand grabbed his arm. Alfie gave a small yelp, but as the hand pulled him into an alleyway, a cold finger was pressed against his lips . . . Daisy!

'What –' Alfie started to say, but a door opened and Daisy quickly pushed him inside, with Rascal right behind them.

Chapter 9

MARCH 1912

'Drop the hammer down there,' Daisy told Alfie, moving a thick mat aside and pulling up a small trap door in the floor.

Alfie dropped it on top of a pile of other toffee hammers, bricks, stones, ornaments and Indian clubs. The room they had taken refuge in had no furniture, just the thick mats on the floor, and it smelt faintly of sweat. There were five women wearing exercise clothes: red crossover jackets and knee-length trousers over their black stockings. Alfie felt a bit embarrassed. Why were the ladies dressed like this? He tried not to stare at them.

'Take your shoes off,' Daisy said.

Alfie did so, only to look up in horror as Daisy started pulling off her own clothes.

'What?'

Underneath her clothes Daisy was wearing the same wrap top and short trousers as the other women.

'What's that boy doing here?' asked a tiny fierce-looking lady, who was obviously in charge.

'Please, Mrs Garrud – he's my brother and Mrs Pankhurst's messenger boy. If the police catch him, he'll be arrested . . .' Daisy said.

But Mrs Garrud had now spotted an even more unusual visitor.

'And is that Mrs Pankhurst's messenger dog?' she asked, as Rascal came out from behind Alfie's legs wagging her tail.

'Yes, ma'am,' Alfie said.

'Mrs Garrud, or *Sensei* – that means "teacher" – will do. And you are both welcome at my *dojo* – this space where I teach.' The tiny woman laughed.

Just then there was a loud thumping at the door.

'Places, ladies,' Mrs Garrud said, and Daisy and the other women ran to the mats and started throwing each other to the floor. More thumps at the door, more insistent now.

'Open up, in the name of the law!' a man's voice shouted.

'Just coming,' Mrs Garrud called out. She looked at Alfie and Rascal and pointed to a bamboo screen with an oriental painting on it in the corner of the room. Alfie nodded and ran to hide behind the screen with Rascal. Rascal sniffed at the bamboo and then gave it a lick.

'We have reason to believe you're hiding some of the vandals who broke shop windows along Oxford Street,' Alfie heard a policeman tell Mrs Garrud when she opened the door. 'May we come in?'

'It wouldn't be proper. I've got ladies here having a jiu-jitsu lesson. They're not dressed for male company. I don't expect gentlemen to come in . . .'

'We're not gentlemen, we're the police, and we have reason to believe you're harbouring criminals,' the policeman replied.

'Very well, come in if you must. You won't find anything,' Mrs Garrud said. 'But take your shoes off. No one wears shoes in this *dojo*.'

Alfie gulped. He could feel his heart beating fast in his chest. He heard Mrs Garrud close the door as the policemen came in.

'Look wherever you like, but I have to get back to my lesson,' she said.

Alfie found a tiny gap between two of the bamboo panels of the screen. He positioned his eye against it and watched as the policemen started searching the room.

'The most common bone that gets broken is the collarbone, and that's because people fall wrongly,' Mrs Garrud told the women. 'So the first thing you need to learn is how to fall properly so that you don't get injured. I want you to bend one knee, put your other leg up and roll back on to the mat on your shoulders. As you land, slap down on the mat with your hand slightly cupped.'

Slap, slap, slap went the women's hands on the mats as they practised falling. Rascal looked up at Alfie and started panting.

Alfie stroked her furry head to comfort her.

Mrs Garrud continued to teach her lesson while the policemen searched the room and the women got in their way. 'If an attacker

had you in a bear hug, what would you do?'
Mrs Garrud asked as one of the officers
checked inside a laundry basket.

'Scream blue murder,' said Daisy, and the
other women laughed.

'Or you could do this,' Mrs Garrud said.
'Would you mind, dear?' she asked the young
policeman, who put the lid back on the
laundry basket.

'Oh – not at all,' he said, looking embarrassed.

'What's your name?' Mrs Garrud asked him.

'Police Constable Smith,' the young officer
said.

'Grab me in a bear hug – from behind, if
you don't mind, PC Smith,' Mrs Garrud told
him. 'Pin my arms tightly to my side so I can't
escape.'

Alfie watched as Constable Smith hesitantly
put his arms round Mrs Garrud, with Daisy,
the other women and the policemen watching.

Fast as lightning, before the officer even realized what was happening, Mrs Garrud dipped down low to the ground so her arms were no longer pinned to her sides. Then she turned, grabbed the policeman's shoulder and arm, twisted round so her hip was against his, and the next moment he lost his balance and landed flat on his back on the mat. He sat up with a surprised look on his face.

How on earth had she done that? Alfie wondered.

Daisy ran forward to help the young officer up.

'Thank you,' he said, his face red with embarrassment. 'I don't know quite how that happened.'

Alfie recognized him as the police officer who had pushed him out of the way of the police horses the day he'd met Rascal.

Daisy smiled as Constable Smith scratched his head and looked round at the women, who were applauding Mrs Garrud.

Rascal had had enough of hiding. She poked her nose out from behind the screen to see what all the fuss was about. Alfie leapt forward to pull her back into their hiding place, but his heart stopped as he locked eyes with the young policeman – they had been spotted!

'I can't find anything here,' the young officer told the other policemen, turning away. 'We should keep looking elsewhere.'

Alfie slipped back behind the screen and breathed a sigh of relief when he heard Mrs Garrud open the door and the police took their leave.

As the door closed behind them, Mrs Garrud let out a big laugh, and the other women laughed too.

'That showed them!'

She beckoned to Alfie to come out from behind the screen so he and Rascal could watch the rest of the class.

'It's hard enough fighting other women who are of similar height and weight to you in the *dojo*. But soon you'll have to use your new jiu-jitsu fighting skills out on the streets, against men who've been taught to fight, maybe with sticks and knives,' Mrs Garrud said.

Alfie and Rascal watched as Daisy and the other women were taught to use parasols as weapons as well as Indian clubs that were similar to police batons.

'Work in pairs now,' Mrs Garrud told everyone. 'Fighting skills. Remember, you have to get close to the attacker sometimes before you can unbalance them. Use that imbalance to defeat them, giving you or the person you're protecting the chance to run away.'

'But would it really work against a big strong man?' a short, red-haired girl asked. 'That policeman wasn't trying to fight.'

'Even better – if you do it properly and practise the technique until you're lightning quick and he doesn't know what's coming, Maud,' Mrs Garrud said.

'Just like with that policeman,' laughed Daisy.

'I let him down easily,' Mrs Garrud told her. 'Most men won't expect us to be able to defend ourselves or anyone else, and that's where we'll have the advantage.'

Maud didn't have anyone to practise with, so Mrs Garrud asked Alfie to join in and make a pair.

'You're about the same height,' she said. All of the partners bowed to each other before they began to fight.

Alfie didn't know what he was supposed to do, but Maud did. She grabbed hold of Alfie, threw him to the floor and was just about to kick him when Rascal ran on to the mat and started barking at her.

'Stop it, you silly dog,' Maud said.

But Rascal didn't stop until Alfie said: 'It's OK, Rascal, I'm all right. It's OK.'

Mrs Garrud had seen what had happened and was cross with Maud.

'You must learn not to use excessive force when you're practising in the *dojo*. True martial artists do not strike hard just for the sake of it. They use their skill, and you should use yours and treat your opponent with respect.'

'Sorry, Alfie,' Maud said, as she helped him up. 'I got carried away.'

'See you next week,' Mrs Garrud said, at the end of the lesson. 'And if you get a chance to practise at home, please do so. It all helps.'

Alfie, Daisy and Rascal were the last to leave because they helped to put the mats against the wall ready for next time.

'My bicycle!' Alfie exclaimed when they went out. There it was, propped up against the wall, and it still had Rascal's ball in the basket. With it was a note and an apple. The note said: 'Sorry I had to borrow it. But here it is, as good as new.' The note wasn't signed. But Alfie didn't care. He was overjoyed to have his bicycle back. Now he could carry on taking messages for Mrs Pankhurst and the WSPU – it was so much quicker to deliver them by bike.

'Edith – I mean Mrs Garrud – is one of the very first professional martial-arts instructors in the Western world,' Daisy told Alfie as they headed home. 'Lots of suffragettes go there to learn self-defence. They've been putting cardboard under their clothes to protect them against being punched, but it isn't enough – we need to be able to fight back. Edith's going to give extra training to the thirty best jiu-jitsuists among us. Those thirty will become Mrs Pankhurst's chosen bodyguards.'

From the way Daisy's eyes sparkled, Alfie was pretty sure his sister wanted to be one of them.

Chapter 10

1912

The next morning, Saturday, Mr Goulden told Alfie and Daisy that Mrs Pankhurst had been arrested for throwing stones through the windows of 10 Downing Street.

Alfie looked at Daisy and bit his bottom lip. He'd almost been arrested too, but he didn't tell Mr and Mrs Goulden that.

There'd been so many arrests after the window smashing in London that the court had to sit for the whole of Saturday, and even by the end of the day only thirteen of the 122 cases had been heard.

'The damage is estimated at five thousand pounds,' Mr Goulden told them.

Alfie was worried about Miss Billinghurst. Maybe if he hadn't picked up the toffee hammer, the police wouldn't have seen that she had lots of them hidden under her blanket and wouldn't have arrested her. Many of the women were sentenced to at least four months in prison, some with hard labour. Alfie was relieved when he learnt that Miss Billinghurst had only been given one month, without any hard labour.

The suffragettes were some of the bravest women in Britain, Alfie thought, as he watched his sister trying to perfect her break-falls and parasol-swinging so that Mrs Garrud would choose her to be one of Mrs Pankhurst's bodyguards. But they were also some of the most stubborn!

On the day of Mrs Pankhurst's release, in June, Daisy, Rascal and Alfie went to meet her and helped her into the WSPU car.

Mrs Pankhurst was very weak and shaking with cold. She'd refused to eat or drink anything for the last five days. Although Alfie could remember being hungry in the workhouse a long, long time ago, he'd never been hungry since. It was hard to imagine how not eating for days and days would feel. He was pretty sure Rascal wouldn't like it one bit – she was a dog who loved her food, plus any extra bits she could find or beg for. Alfie knew most days she'd happily eat his food as well as her own. She'd never last on a hunger strike, especially if people came into her cell with tempting dishes. But somehow Mrs Pankhurst, and many of the other suffragettes, had done it.

Mrs Pankhurst looked really ill, though: her skin had a yellow tinge and there was a sickly sweet smell coming from her. Alfie was very worried about her. He wished she didn't have to go on hunger strike but he knew there was no point telling her not to. Mrs Pankhurst had very strong opinions, and one boy and his dog weren't going to change them!

In the back of the car Rascal cuddled up to Mrs Pankhurst, who seemed only half-conscious, and gave her a lick to comfort her as they drove to 2 Campden Hill Square, the home of Mrs Brackenbury, a suffragette who was eighty years old. Mrs Brackenbury and her two daughters were passionate supporters of Mrs Pankhurst and the Votes for Women cause, and

Mrs Brackenbury had also been sent to prison, for two weeks, for breaking two windows in Whitehall.

When the car finally pulled up outside the house, Nurse Pine and Mrs Brackenbury came out to help Mrs Pankhurst inside.

'Oh, you poor dear,' Mrs Brackenbury said. 'You poor, poor dear.'

'It's not me you should worry about,' Mrs Pankhurst whispered, resting on their arms for support. 'It's the other women who are still in prison, still going through this, some of them being force-fed. The individual will disappear, but the fight for the cause must go on.'

Alfie looked over at the policemen standing on the road outside the house. They always followed Mrs Pankhurst and the leading members of the WSPU to keep an eye on the suffragettes.

Constable Tom Smith didn't see Alfie looking at him, but he knew that he and the other police weren't wanted there.

'Come on inside,' Mrs Brackenbury said to Mrs Pankhurst. 'And I'll get you a nice cup of tea.'

It was important Mrs Pankhurst didn't eat solid food too soon after her hunger strike or she'd be sick.

'Camomile,' Mrs Pankhurst whispered.

'Yes, camomile,' said her friend Ethel Smyth. 'With a little peppermint.'

Mrs Pankhurst couldn't even manage to walk without the help of other people. Was it really worth all this to get the vote? Alfie wasn't sure, although he was sure that having the vote would be a very good thing. And Mrs Pankhurst would say it was certainly worth it. Anything was worth it for the cause.

Rascal sat down next to Mrs Pankhurst's bed and Mrs Pankhurst's hand rested softly on her fur.

'You and your dog bring such comfort,' Mrs Brackenbury said to Alfie. 'Can you stay for a while?'

'We could do with your nursing skills,' Nurse Pine said to Daisy. 'More and more sick women are going to be brought here from prison over the next few days and weeks.'

Daisy and Alfie wanted to help and said they could stay. Rascal was kept busy being stroked.

When she was well enough, Mrs Pankhurst packed to go to France to see Christabel, her eldest daughter, who'd escaped there before she could be arrested.

'She has a dog too,' Mrs Pankhurst told Rascal as she packed a few belongings.

'I expect the two of you would get along very well. Her name's Fay and she's a Pomeranian, just like your friends, Princess Sophia's dogs.'

Rascal sat on the doorstep with Alfie to watch as Mrs Pankhurst was driven away in the WSPU car.

'Walkies?' Alfie said. Rascal wagged her tail enthusiastically and raced back inside to fetch her ball.

The houses in Campden Hill Square were built round a communal garden, but there weren't usually any other dogs there besides Rascal. Not that she minded too much – she had her ball and Alfie to play with, and squirrels and pigeons to chase.

Rascal was very interested in the young policeman on duty outside Mrs Brackenbury's front garden when they got back. She wagged her tail at him.

'Come on, Rascal,' Alfie said, looking down at the ground. He didn't want to talk to the police and he didn't want them stroking Rascal. She'd got her purple, white and green collar on and she was a suffragette mascot, not a police dog.

In the afternoon, while Alfie was busy doing the schoolwork Mrs Goulden had sent for him, Rascal picked up her ball and slipped outside.

'Well, hello there,' Constable Tom Smith said.

Rascal dropped her ball at his feet and looked up expectantly at him, her brown eyes willing him to pick it up.

Tom had been sent to keep an eye on the suffragettes but no one had said anything about whether he should or shouldn't play with a dog while he was there. He quickly looked round to make sure no one was watching, then he picked up the ball and threw it for Rascal.

With a wag of her tail Rascal ran across the lawn to fetch the ball. She brought it back to him, dropped it at his feet and looked up at him, ready to go again.

Alfie wondered why Rascal was panting when she came in an hour later, but he had a lot to do and so he didn't think much about it. Rascal dropped her ball in her basket and had a long drink of water.

'Alfie, can you give me a hand?' Daisy shouted. She wanted to set up a ramp by the front steps so Miss Billinghurst could come in and out as she pleased once she was released from prison.

'Coming,' Alfie called.

Rascal picked up her ball and headed back out of the front door, but the policeman who had played with her wasn't there any more. The new policeman shooed her away, so she headed back indoors for a nap.

She was so pleased when the friendly policeman came back early the next morning that she rolled over on her back for him to give her a tummy rub.

'Well, I missed you too,' Constable Tom said. The truth was that playing with the dog had been the highlight of the previous day.

He threw the ball across the grass in front of the house for Rascal but quickly returned to his post by the garden wall when Miss Billinghurst's carriage arrived.

Rascal didn't want to stop playing. She dropped her ball at Tom's feet and held out her paw.

'Not now,' Tom whispered, before quickly standing to attention. He knew he shouldn't let the suffragettes see him playing with one of their dogs!

'Where's Rascal? I want to give her a pet,' Miss Billinghurst said, as Alfie and Daisy came out of the house to help her inside.

'Rascal!' Alfie called.

He spotted her sitting next to the policeman on duty by the garden wall.

'Rascal – come here.'

She picked up her ball and came running over to Alfie.

'Hello, there,' Miss Billinghurst said, giving her a stroke.

Rascal wagged her tail and rubbed her face against Miss Billinghurst's hand. Alfie was glad she didn't try to jump up on Miss Billinghurst's lap, as she'd done when she was a puppy. She was so much bigger and heavier now.

'It's wonderful to be out of prison and free to have a cuddle with my favourite dog,' Miss Billinghurst said.

'How about a nice cup of tea?' Daisy asked her.

'Yes, please,' Miss Billinghurst said. 'And then I'm looking forward to having a long sleep in a non-prison bed.'

Alfie still felt guilty about picking up the toffee hammer but Miss Billinghurst told him he shouldn't.

'If the police hadn't arrested me then, I'd have just kept on breaking more and more windows until they did!' she said.

Chapter 11

1912–13

Rascal loved going for long walks but Alfie thought even she would struggle to walk as far as some of the suffragettes had done during their Votes for Women campaign. Suffragettes from Wales had walked from Bangor to London. Suffragettes from Cornwall had walked from Land's End to London. And now six suffragettes from Scotland had walked four hundred miles from Edinburgh to London.

'Come on, Rascal,' Alfie said, and Rascal grabbed her ball off the balcony at Lincoln's Inn House, the headquarters of the WSPU since October 1912. These headquarters were much bigger, and they needed to be: the WSPU had grown so big that it now employed over a hundred people, including Daisy and Alfie, who both worked for it full time. They lived in the small caretaker's flat at the top of the building with Rascal.

Rascal's favourite spot in their new home was the balcony. She liked to sit out on it and watch the people and other dogs and cats passing by down below.

'We're not going out to play,' Alfie said, when he saw Rascal pick up her ball.

But Rascal gave him a look that said she didn't want to put it down.

Alfie sighed. 'All right, bring it if you must, but we won't be playing.'

There were hundreds of other well-wishers at Trafalgar Square waiting to cheer the Scottish suffragettes from the Women's Freedom League as they arrived.

'Four hundred miles,' Alfie kept thinking. Would he walk four hundred miles to get the right to vote? Maybe. Although Mrs Pankhurst didn't just want women to get the vote – she wanted them to have equal rights with men.

'I wore my shoe leather out,' one of the women, Nannie Brown, told Alfie in her soft Scottish voice. Rascal looked up at her, dropped her ball at Nannie's feet, and then picked it up again when Nannie didn't throw it for her. 'It took us five whole weeks to walk here, fifteen miles every day, rain or shine, and we collected thousands of signatures in support of women's right to vote along the way. Now we want to show it to the prime minister. Surely Mr Asquith will see that he must give us the vote now.'

Alfie and Rascal went with them to 10 Downing Street. But when the women knocked on the door with their petition, the prime minister refused to see them and they had to give it to one of his secretaries instead.

'We've come so far . . .' Nannie said, as she handed it over to the stony-faced man in the grey suit who blocked the doorway.

Alfie felt really sorry for the women. Why wouldn't Mr Asquith just see them? Alfie thought it was the least he could do.

Rascal looked over at St James's Park as they passed it on their way back from Downing Street. Then she stopped, sat down, dropped her ball on the ground and looked up at Alfie.

'OK,' Alfie sighed. At least someone would get what they wanted from the trip to 10 Downing Street today.

Rascal ran into the park and Alfie threw the ball for her over and over again, then they headed back to Lincoln's Inn House. Rascal had a nice sleep in the wintry sunshine on the balcony, before heading back in for her dinner.

Alfie and Rascal were in the WSPU offices a few months later when a lady with a shawl round her shoulders and clogs on her feet walked through the door.

'Annie!' Alfie said, smiling. 'Why are you dressed in your old mill worker's clothes today?'

He'd never forgotten meeting Annie Kenney the first time in Manchester when he and Daisy had escaped from the workhouse. She was wearing the same clothes as she had been then. But she'd never gone back to working in the mill.

Annie Kenney had worked all over England for the WSPU and often went to France to report to Mrs Pankhurst's daughter Christabel. Now she was in charge of the WSPU in London.

Rascal liked Annie very much and nudged her head under her hand for a stroke.

'Me and some other working women – twenty of us, including Flora Drummond – have got a meeting with David Lloyd George, the Chancellor of the Exchequer,' Annie told him excitedly. 'It's not the prime minister – he wouldn't see us – but it's almost as good. The chancellor's on our side and one day – well, who knows? – he could become prime minister and things will change.'

Rascal greeted the other women as they arrived at Lincoln's Inn to practise what they were going to say at the meeting with Lloyd George. There were school teachers, nurses, mill hands and laundresses, pit brow women who worked in the coal mines, and fisherwomen – twenty working women from all over the country to represent all the hundreds of thousands of working women.

When Flora Drummond arrived, Rascal put her paw out to her and The General gave her a stroke.

'Now, ladies,' she said, as Alfie handed round cups of tea and scones. 'The vote is the best way we can get our views listened to. Tell us what you would each like to say to Lloyd George.'

Mrs Hawkins, who was representing working mothers, said: 'Mothers need the vote so that they can demand better, safer homes for their families, medical treatment for all, and good schooling for both their sons and their daughters. My two sons – one in the Army and one in the Navy – have the vote, yet the woman who brought them into the world has no say.'

Mrs Bonnick, the headmistress of a London school, wanted to speak about the rights of women teachers: 'They should have the same pay and voting power as male teachers have.'

Sister Townsend, a hospital nurse, said she represented women whose hours were longer than those of any male worker. 'We don't just work as hard – we work harder, and yet we're refused the right to vote and expected to pay taxes without any say in what those taxes will be used for.'

Annie looked over at Alfie and smiled and he smiled back. Surely the government would finally see sense and give women the vote now?

Annie came back disappointed after the meeting with Lloyd George.

'I don't know,' she said, as Alfie took her shawl. 'The chancellor said he'd pass on our words, but I don't hold out much hope until Mr Asquith isn't in power any more.'

'I don't trust any of them,' The General said.

They had Emily Wilding Davison with them, although she hadn't been part of the group meeting Lloyd George. Rascal and Emily were old friends because she often popped into the office.

'We have to do more,' Emily said as she gave Rascal a tummy rub. Emily was good at finding Rascal's tickle spot, which made her hind left leg wave wildly in the air. 'We have to do something huge to make the government give us the right to vote. Something they can't ignore.'

Chapter 12

June 1913

It was a sunny Wednesday and Alfie was helping in the typing room at Lincoln's Inn House, laboriously typing letters with one finger, when Emily Davison came rushing in.

'Good morning, Miss Davison,' Alfie said, as Rascal trotted over to her and rubbed her face against Emily's skirt.

'I want two Votes for Women flags,' she said.

Alfie got two of the purple, white and green flags from the cupboard and gave them to her.

Emily was tingling with excitement. Rascal decided she must want to play so she fetched her ball and dropped it at Emily's feet.

'Oh, no, sorry – I don't have time to play now. I'm off to Epsom to see the races,' Emily told her. 'I'm going to watch the Derby.'

Alfie thought how lucky Emily was. How he'd love to watch the racing!

'The king's horse, Anmer, is running in the Derby today,' Alfie told Emily. He'd seen a picture of the beautiful bay horse, with its reddish-brown body and black mane, tail, ear edges and lower legs. It would be wonderful to see it race.

'I know,' Emily told him with a small smile.

Rascal nudged Emily's hand with her head, put out her paw and looked up at Emily.

'Oh, all right,' Emily said. 'Who could resist you?' And she gave Rascal one of her favourite tummy rubs before running off down the winding staircase.

'Emily!' Daisy called after her, pulling open a desk drawer. 'I just remembered – this came for you a few days ago.'

But Emily had already gone.

'I hope it's not urgent,' Daisy said, staring at the envelope with 'Miss Wilding Davison' written on it.

'I'll run and catch her,' Alfie said, grabbing the envelope and tearing off down the stairs with Rascal right behind him.

But when they got outside, the street was so crowded that Alfie couldn't see Emily anywhere.

'Well, we know where she's going,' Alfie told Rascal as he took his bicycle from the bike rack and held it steady so Rascal could hop into the basket.

It took almost two hours to cycle to Epsom but Alfie didn't mind a bit. It was a beautiful summer's day and he was going to the Derby after all!

Rascal didn't mind either, although she didn't have her ball.

Alfie had never been to a racecourse before. He paid two shillings for their ticket and they were allowed in. Rascal was very interested in all the horsey smells, but when she saw a horse towering above her, she trembled with fear.

'It's OK,' Alfie told her, as he stroked the horse's nose. 'He won't hurt you.'

Rascal sniffed at the horse and it put its nose down to her and breathed out through its nostrils, ruffling her fur.

'Nice dog,' said the jockey.

'Thanks!' Alfie grinned.

More people came to stroke Rascal and she happily wagged her tail, especially when someone gave her a bit of jellied eel.

As well as the horses and jockeys, there were thousands of spectators dressed in their best clothes – and of course the king and queen were in the Royal Box. Alfie wasn't sure how he was ever going to find Miss Davison among all the people and horses and fairground stalls and rides.

He spotted a lady who looked a little bit like her over by the steam carousel, waiting to ride on one of the wooden horses, but Emily had said she was there to watch the racing.

As he searched the face of every woman he passed, he thought about how Emily was one of the bravest of the suffragettes. One time she had even managed to stay hidden in the House of Commons overnight – until she'd been found and sent to prison. Mrs Pankhurst said Emily Davison was now in the House of Commons' black book – for people who weren't welcome there any more.

Alfie thought Mrs Pankhurst was probably in the black book too.

'Lucky heather?' a little girl with bare feet asked him, holding out a small bunch of purple flowers.

Alfie shook his head and walked on. He had to find Miss Davison.

'Come on, Rascal,' he called.

Rascal had never smelt anything quite like the scent at the edge of the racecourse. It was so good it was impossible to resist – she kept her nose to the ground and trotted over to the other side of the racecourse, away from the crowds of people's feet, to follow it.

'Rascal!' Alfie called, but Rascal didn't even lift her head.

One minute Rascal had been right next to Alfie, and the next she was gone.

'Rascal – Rascal, where are you?' he called.

All around him people were shouting. Some wanted people to bet on the horses, some wanted people to have a go on the fairground stalls and rides, others had food and souvenirs to sell.

Alfie thought the racecourse was just about the worst place for Rascal to get lost. There were so many people going this way and that. Rascal would surely get lost in the crowds in no time. Not to mention the danger of the horses' hooves.

'Rascal!'

There were no people once Rascal crossed the stretch of grass on the other side of the racecourse. Only the woods just ahead, where the scent that filled Rascal's nostrils was taking her. She trotted on and was thrilled to come face to face with a fox! It ventured out of its den and looked at her as Rascal wagged her tail.

'Rascal! Rascal!' Alfie shouted as loudly as he could and Rascal heard him. When she turned her head and whined, the fox disappeared back into its den. All that was left was the fox's scat. Rascal rolled over and over in it with her legs in the air and then she pressed her face into it. Finally she raced back to Alfie, as pleased as could be with her new aroma.

'Yuck, Rascal,' Alfie said, once he'd hugged her. 'You smell terrible!' He knew it wasn't horse manure, but it wasn't like anything else he'd smelt before either – a sour, almost a foul, cheesy kind of smell. 'What have you been rolling in?'

Rascal wagged her tail.

By the time they got back to the course, the Derby was over. Alfie still hadn't seen Emily.

'She's probably gone home by now,' he told Rascal.

'Did the king's horse win?' he asked a man selling Lyons ice cream from a handcart.

'No, Craganour won but got disqualified, so it was given to Aboyeur instead. There was an incident on the track but Anmer's not injured.'

'What happened?' Alfie asked, pulling some money from his pocket and buying the

cheapest ice cream the man had for sale.
Rascal hadn't tasted ice cream before.

Alfie had a lick before he gave some to Rascal.
Rascal lapped it up, then looked up for more.

'Anmer was coming almost last, only a few
horses after him, when a woman ran on to the
track and got herself knocked over,' the man
said.

'Is she OK?' Alfie asked, as Rascal licked
the melting ice cream dripping from the cone
in his hand.

The man shook his head.

'She's been taken to hospital. Can't think
why she did something so foolish. Someone
said she was one of those suffs . . . sufferers?
Women who want the vote.'

Alfie froze. 'You mean suffragettes,' he said,
with a feeling of dread rising in his chest.

Miss Davison was always saying something
extreme needed to be done to draw attention

to the cause of women's suffrage. But she wouldn't have run out on to the racecourse, would she? She wouldn't have done that, Alfie told himself. But a tiny voice inside his head said she might have.

'They say the injuries looked very grave,' the man added.

Alfie *had* to find out what had happened. He ran over to the nearest policeman.

'Do you know the name of the woman who was knocked over by the horse, sir?' he asked.

The policeman pulled out his notebook and looked at it.

'A Miss Wilding Davison,' he told him.

Alfie knew he had to let the WSPU headquarters know what had happened as soon as possible. Not many houses had telephones yet. But he bet a princess's house would have one. And Hampton Court was much nearer than London.

Alfie grabbed his bike.

'Up, Rascal.'

Rascal jumped into her basket and Alfie pedalled as fast as he could to find Princess Sophia.

The further away from the racecourse he got, the guiltier he felt. Maybe if he had found Miss Davison, given her the letter, he might have been able to stop her from doing something so rash. Maybe.

Hampton Court Palace had been closed to the public in February 'owing to fear of damage by women suffragists' and there were extra policemen guarding it, but on the road outside Alfie saw Princess Sophia selling copies of the WSPU newspaper, *The Suffragette*.

'Votes for Women!' the princess shouted as she rang a handbell. 'Votes for Women!'

The people walking past did not look very pleased with the bell ringing or the shouting.

Alfie squeezed the bicycle's brakes as he skidded to a stop beside her.

'Alfie?' the princess said, when she saw him.

Rascal jumped out of her basket and ran over to be stroked.

'What on earth are you doing here?' the princess asked.

'Miss Davison,' Alfie gasped. 'Ran in front of the king's horse, Anmer, at the Derby.'

'Oh, no! Is she all right?' the princess asked, her hand going to her throat and deep worry lines appearing on her brow.

Alfie shook his head. 'I don't think so. She's been taken to Epsom hospital. We have to let the WSPU London office know.'

'Come back with me to Faraday House,' the princess said. 'I can telephone them from there.'

Manna was in the kitchen.

'Alfie!' he said, his face breaking into a huge grin when he saw him.

'Alfie needs some mint tea with lots of honey and Rascal some water,' the princess said. Manna hurried to make the tea while the princess went to telephone Lincoln's Inn House.

'Maybe if I'd got there earlier I could have stopped her – could have done something,' Alfie said. It all felt so hopeless.

'It wasn't your fault,' Manna told him. 'Truly it wasn't. You weren't to know what she planned to do.'

But Alfie still felt terrible.

Four days later there was a telephone call to the WSPU headquarters at Lincoln's Inn House: Miss Davison had not survived her injuries.

A suffragette named Miss Roe organized the funeral and Alfie and Rascal followed the five thousand women who marched in the solemn funeral procession to Bloomsbury. Some of the ladies wore black and carried purple irises; some wore white and held white lilies. Silent crowds watched on the pavements as the procession marched past.

Emily Wilding Davison's coffin was draped in a purple cloth with two broad white arrows. The arrows were a reminder of the many times she'd been sent to prison for the suffragettes' cause.

Was having the vote worth Miss Davison's life? Alfie wondered, as he remembered Emily laughing and giving Rascal a tummy rub. But in his heart he knew she would have thought it was worth dying for. Now, surely, women's right to vote would be taken seriously by everyone. The story of Emily's death was in the newspapers all over the world.

In the procession was a carriage for Mrs Pankhurst, but Mrs Pankhurst wasn't in it. The moment she'd left her flat with her daughter Sylvia and Nurse Pine to join the funeral, she'd been arrested by the police.

Chapter 13

1914

'I'm in!' Daisy announced one late January morning when Alfie came into the tiny kitchen of their flat at the WSPU headquarters. Her smile was huge.

'In what?' Alfie asked her, while Rascal sniffed the air.

'Mrs Pankhurst's bodyguard,' Daisy told him, putting a plate of crumpets on the table in front of Alfie. She gave Rascal one of the crumpets that she'd made to celebrate.

As soon as she'd gulped it down, Rascal looked up, licking her lips and hoping for some more.

'Good for you!' Alfie told his sister.

Daisy had been working at her jiu-jitsu for months and months, hoping Mrs Garrud would pick her. Sometimes she practised with Alfie but mostly she used the hatstand in the hallway or practised break-falls on the bed.

'Nearly at Mouse Castle,' Daisy said a few evenings later as they travelled in the back of the WSPU car.

'Why are you calling it that?' Alfie asked her. They'd often been to Mrs Brackenbury's house before and he'd never seen a mouse there.

'Rascal's good at catching mice,' he said, and Rascal, who was on the floor next to Alfie's feet, looked up.

'No, that's not why it's got the name,' Daisy said, lowering her voice as she looked over at Mrs Pankhurst, who'd only just been released from prison again and appeared to be asleep. 'It's because of the Cat and Mouse Act that was passed by Parliament. Suffragette prisoners who go on hunger strike are allowed to go free until they've built up their strength, then they'll get re-arrested as soon as they're strong enough to go back to prison and finish their sentence.'

Alfie looked over at Mrs Pankhurst's pale, exhausted face. The government was playing with the suffragette prisoners like a cat with a mouse. By letting them out of prison when they were weak and putting them back when they'd recovered a little, the government was like a cat torturing a mouse.

'We'll triumph in the end because we have right on our side,' Mrs Pankhurst said, as

Alfie, Daisy and Nurse Pine helped her to her room, where Dr Flora Murray was waiting. Rascal ran ahead and lay down next to Mrs Pankhurst's bed so she'd be there, ready to be stroked, when Mrs Pankhurst needed her.

Once Mrs Pankhurst was feeling a bit better she wanted to be moved from Mouse Castle.

'Having the police here all the time is too stressful for the other suffragettes trying to recover,' she said. 'And wherever I am the police follow these days, waiting to re-arrest me.'

If they saw she was strong enough to leave Mouse Castle, they'd put her back in prison.

'You have to stay here,' Dr Murray said.

But when Mrs Pankhurst wanted something done, she usually wanted it done straight away. So Alfie was sent to the editor of the *Globe* in Fleet Street with Mrs Pankhurst's written announcement in time for the evening edition:

This evening Mrs Pankhurst will be speaking at a public open-air meeting at Campden Hill Square.

'What's going on?' Alfie asked when he got back. There was something different about Daisy. From the strange way she was smiling, it was as if she had a secret she was bursting to tell him but wasn't allowed to.

'Nothing,' she said.

'Right,' said Alfie. He could always tell when Daisy wasn't telling him the whole truth.

Rascal stood on her hind legs and had a quick lick of the plates that had been left on the table before Daisy saw her and told her to get down.

The evening edition of the *Globe* was printed at 5 p.m. and available for people to buy from 6 p.m. A little later Alfie looked out of the window and saw people arriving to hear Mrs Pankhurst speak.

'Come on, Rascal,' Alfie said, and they went down to join the crowd.

Outside Rascal immediately started wagging her tail and trotted over to a lady in a fur coat with her back to them.

'Rascal, come back!' Alfie called, but then the lady turned and he realized it was Princess Sophia.

'Hello, Alfie.' She smiled as he hurried over to her.

'I didn't expect you to be here, your . . . your Highness,' Alfie said.

The princess put her finger to her lips. 'I don't want anyone to know who I am. I came with my friend, Ada Wright.'

Alfie remembered Ada Wright from Black Friday, when Daisy had treated her injuries.

'We thought we'd come and show our support. Mrs Pankhurst is such a fine speaker,' Ada said.

By seven o'clock, there was a crowd of over a thousand pro-suffragists, who wanted women to have the vote, and anti-suffragists, who didn't, crammed into the square. At eight o'clock, a slim figure dressed all in black, and wearing a large fashionable hat with a veil over her face, appeared at the first-floor window.

'There she is,' Alfie said, pointing upward.

Some people cheered and others booed as they too spotted her.

The lady came out and stood on the balcony. Around Alfie the throng hushed as people stared up at the woman in the large hat and veil that hid her face. Alfie frowned. It was Mrs Pankhurst, wasn't it? The crowd pushed forward, trying to get a better look. Around him, Alfie heard people asking the same question.

Rascal whined and Alfie wished he'd left her safely in the house. He didn't want her soft paws getting stepped on by heavy boots. Fortunately the princess and Ada Wright were standing next to Rascal, helping to block people from accidentally treading on her.

The lady lifted her veil and now Alfie could see that she was indeed Mrs Pankhurst.

'Now, my friends, I want to challenge the government . . .' Mrs Pankhurst said. Pro- and anti-suffragists grew quiet as they strained to hear her words. When she said that she refused to be put back in prison to finish her sentence because of the horror of the Cat and Mouse Act, the police tried to push through the crowd of people in the square to arrest her.

But the next moment Alfie saw a dozen women coming out of the front door. In the middle of them was Mrs Pankhurst, dressed all in black with the veil over her face.

The twelve women linked arms and shoved their way through the crowd. Alfie gasped when he saw that one of them was Daisy.

'Help us!' she called to Alfie as the police tried to break the circle and the women struggled to hold on to each other to protect Mrs Pankhurst.

Alfie, Rascal, Princess Sophia and Ada Wright ran forward with other suffragettes to form a second ring outside the first. They too linked arms to stop the police and anti-suffragists from reaching Mrs Parkhurst.

One of the policemen drew out his truncheon and swung it at Daisy.

'We won't let you take her!' Daisy screamed, as she ducked.

Rascal ran at the policeman and started barking and growling.

'No, Rascal,' Alfie said, grabbing her and pulling her away.

If Mrs Pankhurst got arrested, she'd be put back in prison – but a dog that was arrested for showing aggression, even if it was only trying to protect an innocent person, that would be a whole different story.

Rascal broke free from Alfie and dashed over to the policeman now holding the veiled woman in black. She barked and barked.

'Get out of it, dog,' the policeman said, kicking at Rascal.

Another policeman lunged at Rascal, his truncheon swinging.

'Run, Alfie!' the princess cried.

Alfie grabbed Rascal by her collar and ran round to the back of the house and in through the kitchen door, just as a woman in black came down the back stairs, helped by Nurse Pine.

Rascal wagged her tail.

'See you soon, Alfred,' Mrs Pankhurst whispered as Nurse Pine helped her to the waiting WSPU car.

Rascal and Alfie ran up to the first floor and from there they watched as Daisy and some of the other bodyguards pulled out Indian clubs hidden in their long skirts.

But it was no use. The police now had hold of the woman in black and they carried her away.

'They've got her!' Daisy said, in tears, when she came back. But Alfie shook his head.

'No, they haven't,' he told her.

Alfie found out the next day that the decoy pretending to be Mrs Pankhurst was a fifty-seven-year-old suffragette called Florence Evelyn Smith.

Both Ada Wright and the princess were arrested, along with lots of other women. But only Ada Wright and six others were sent to prison.

'It's not fair,' the princess told Alfie at the WSPU headquarters. 'Ada shouldn't be suffering in prison while I'm free. I'm going to pay her fine and set her free, even though she won't like it one little bit, and I want to make a donation to the WSPU too.'

She gave Alfie fifty pounds for the WSPU, then she added a one-pound note to it.

'For good luck.'

And then she gave Alfie two more pennies.

'One for you and one . . .'

'To spend on Rascal,' Alfie grinned.

Once Mrs Pankhurst had left Campden Hill Square, Rascal spent more time visiting the other suffragette 'mice' staying at Mouse Castle.

'It's as if your little dog knows what an important role she has, Alfie,' said Dr Murray as she watched the women petting Rascal. 'The children at my Women's Hospital for Children would love her.'

Alfie felt very proud of Rascal and thought she'd like to be petted by the children at the hospital, which had been set up by Dr Murray and her friend Dr Louisa Garrett Anderson for poor children. Its motto was 'Deeds not Words', just like the WSPU's.

'When would you like us to come?' he asked, and Rascal looked up at Dr Murray and wagged her tail.

Daisy's next mission was a month later. As one of Mrs Pankhurst's thirty bodyguards, or 'Amazons' as they were being called in the press, she had to travel all the way to Scotland, where Mrs Pankhurst was due to give a speech. Alfie and Rascal went with Daisy on the train.

'We look much less suspicious as a family group,' she said, as people petted Rascal and said what a good dog she was. 'But make sure you don't join in, Alfie, or let Rascal try to protect me if it gets at all rowdy. I don't want you to get hurt, and we can't afford to have you arrested. Mrs Pankhurst would never forgive me if I got her messenger boy and dog sent to prison.'

Mrs Pankhurst was still on the run from the police after her speech in Campden Hill Square in February, so there were bound to be police trying to catch her at the meeting in Glasgow. But Mrs Pankhurst had said she would speak there and she was determined to keep her word.

When they arrived at St Andrew's Hall in Glasgow on 9 March 1914, Rascal sniffed at the pots of flowers that surrounded the stage.

'Don't let her put her nose too close,' The General warned Alfie. She looked terrifically fierce in her favourite red military coat. 'Those flowers look pretty but they've got barbed wire hidden inside them. If the police storm the stage to arrest Mrs Pankhurst, they'll know all about it.'

Shortly after Mrs Pankhurst began speaking to the audience of five thousand, the police rushed the platform. Alfie was shocked to hear a shot ring out. He looked up to see one of the suffragettes holding a revolver!

'Get out of here, Alfie!' Daisy shouted as she threw flowerpots at the police. 'Get out!'

Alfie grabbed hold of Rascal's collar and pushed his way out through the crowd.

The bodyguards did their best, but Alfie watched as the police came out with Mrs Pankhurst and pushed her into a waiting car.

'They've taken her to the Central Police Office,' a man said, when Daisy came to join Alfie and Rascal. They followed Mrs Pankhurst's supporters to the police station where she was being held. But once they got there, hundreds of police, both on horse and on foot, poured out of the station.

Alfie grabbed Daisy and Rascal and ran as the police scattered people in all directions.

*

'Look, we're even in the paper!' Daisy said proudly the next morning, showing Alfie the headline, MRS PANKHURST'S AMAZONS. 'We'll never give up until the government gives women the vote.'

Alfie was worried. Daisy had a black eye and a cut on her face, and those were the injuries he *could* see. He didn't want his sister getting hurt. They could have all been badly injured last night for nothing. Mrs Pankhurst was still in prison.

But in the summer everything changed.

Chapter 14

1914–18

On 4 August 1914 Britain declared war on Germany.

'Germany's wartime army is 3.7 million. Britain's army has 700,000 available men,' Alfie read in the paper, as Rascal kept dropping her ball beside him, wanting to go out and play.

More, many more, soldiers were needed if Britain was going to win the war, and Alfie wanted to be one of them.

'I'm going to enlist,' he told Manna when he and Rascal went to see him at Faraday House.

'Me too,' Manna said.

But Alfie shook his head.

'You're too young,' he said. Manna was only thirteen.

'So are you,' said Manna. But Alfie was older – fifteen in a few more weeks. 'I don't want to be given one of the white feathers for cowardice,' Manna admitted.

Alfie wished Mrs Pankhurst didn't insist on the suffragettes giving out the white feathers to men who hadn't enlisted yet. Now that she'd called a truce with the government over the Votes for Women issue because of the war, she was determined to get every man to fight and every woman to do her part. The government had let all of the suffragettes out of prison so they could help.

At the recruitment centre in Hampton Town Hall, Alfie just reached the minimum height of five feet three inches. But Manna wasn't five feet yet. He was bitterly disappointed as they headed back to Faraday House with Rascal.

'Alfie's allowed to enlist but I'm not,' Manna told Princess Sophia.

The princess put her hand to her throat.

'Oh, Alfie, are you sure that's a good idea? Your sister will be so worried. And what about dear Rascal? What will she do without you?'

Rascal looked from the princess to Alfie and gave a whine.

'We could look after her!' Manna said. 'They say it will all be over by Christmas, so you'll be back soon, anyway, Alfie.'

The princess nodded. She looked Alfie straight in the eye for a long moment and said: 'You and dear Rascal have made such a big contribution to our efforts. If today is going to be your last day together for a while, it should be a very special day. Has Rascal been to the seaside yet?' she asked.

When Alfie said no, she gave Manna some money for the three of them to go to Brighton.

'I lived there as a child with my sisters and brother,' she said, adding an extra penny to the money. 'On a day like today, there isn't anywhere finer in the world.'

Rascal enjoyed the feel of the pebbles under her feet on Brighton beach, but the sea terrified her. She stared at the vast expanse of water and the waves that came washing in. She gave a bark but the waves didn't stop coming. She gave another bark to tell Alfie to stop putting his toes in the water and then, worse, wading out into the sea. But Alfie didn't stop. Rascal barked again and ran away from the waves to show Alfie what she wanted him to do. Then she stopped and looked back at him. Why didn't he come?

'Come on, Rascal – it's fun!' Alfie called to her.

But Rascal wasn't at all sure about that.

'Let's go right in!' Manna said to Alfie. 'It doesn't matter if our clothes get wet, they'll dry in the sun.'

'I don't want to go in too far,' Alfie said, as Rascal barked at them from the beach.

'Why not?' Manna asked him.

'Because I can't swim!'

'Then you must learn before you go to war, or at least learn how not to drown,' Manna said, scooping up a great armful of water and splashing Alfie with it. Alfie laughed and splashed him back. The two boys were soon in the middle of a wild water fight.

Rascal's head turned from one to the other, then she ran up and down the beach following the flying water. Finally it was too much and she jumped through the waves to try to reach Alfie. The next moment she was swimming and the sea didn't seem quite so bad after all.

She gave the water a quick lap but it didn't taste nice at all.

'Just copy Rascal,' Manna told Alfie, as he watched Rascal doggy-paddling.

Manna held Alfie under his tummy and Alfie stretched his arms out and lifted his legs off the bottom, making sure he kept his head out of the water

'That's it! I won't let you go until you're ready,' said Manna.

Soon Alfie was doggy-paddling like Rascal and laughing at himself – until he gulped down some water by mistake. It might not be great swimming but at least it would stop him from drowning.

Dogs weren't allowed inside the majestic Brighton Pavilion but Rascal was allowed on the pier that stretched far out into the sea.

'One day I will go to India and see a true maharajah's palace for myself,' Manna said.

Through the slatted wooden pier Rascal could see the waves below her, but Alfie didn't seem frightened and so she wasn't frightened either.

Best of all were the fried fish and chips that Manna bought with some of the princess's money. Rascal gobbled hers up and then looked hungrily at the boys' portions. She barked at the seagulls who came to see if there was any for them.

There was just enough time for an ice cream before they had to catch the train. Rascal got to have a whole vanilla ice cream all to herself, which she thought was very fine indeed. Although, once she'd finished hers, she stared meaningfully at Alfie and Manna, who were still eating theirs.

'I don't think Rascal ever gets full up,' Alfie said, as he gave her the last of his ice cream, and Manna laughed.

When they got back to Faraday House, it was time for Alfie to leave Rascal with Manna and Princess Sophia.

'You be good now,' Alfie told Rascal, kissing the top of her furry head. He felt as if his heart was breaking, but he didn't want to seem sad in front of Rascal, because she wouldn't know what was happening or why he was sad, and he wanted her to be happy. 'You're the best dog in the world, you know. But while I'm gone no licking the food from people's plates when they're not looking!'

He was going to miss her so much.

'Take good care of her,' he said to Manna. Although he knew he would.

Alfie ran out to his bicycle and cycled back to London with tears streaming down his face.

The warship taking the soldiers across the sea to France rolled on the swell of the high waves. To the right and left of him Alfie saw and heard other new recruits being seasick. His stomach churned.

'Look towards the horizon,' the soldier standing next to him said, pulling a paper bag of crystallized stem ginger from his pocket and offering it to Alfie. 'Focus on that.'

Alfie took a piece of ginger and sucked on it while doing his best to stare as hard as he could out to sea, but he still felt very sick.

'I'm Tom,' the soldier said. 'Tom Smith. You look familiar. Don't I know you?'

Alfie looked at the man who was a few years older than him and shook his head. He didn't recognize him.

'I'm Alfie,' Alfie gulped.

He was glad Manna had taught him to swim. At least if the ship went down he'd have a chance of surviving. He bit his bottom lip and willed the French coast to appear.

At last they reached dry land and soon the seasickness didn't seem so bad compared with the stench of the muddy, water-logged trenches they had to dig out and live in. Or the threat of attack from the other side that they faced day and night, from both soldiers with weapons and the deadly mustard gas.

When Alfie wrote home he didn't tell Daisy or Manna how bad it truly was in the trenches.

He didn't want them to know about the other soldiers, just like him, some of them not even as old as he was, who'd already been killed or badly injured. There was nothing Daisy or Manna could do to help and he didn't want to worry them. All he could do was see the war through to the end and hopefully, one day, get to go home.

Tom didn't have anyone to write to, so Alfie said he could write to Daisy as well. She was helping Mrs Pankhurst's daughter Sylvia in the East End of London. When war was declared, prices had gone up so much that poor people couldn't afford to buy food and were starving. Sylvia had set up a mother-and-baby clinic, a factory making toys and clothes where unemployed women could work, and a restaurant where meals cost twopence for adults and a penny for children, and you could have a free meal if you had no money at all. Plus it provided soup and a chunk of bread every evening for one penny.

'Good thick soup too – not like we used to have in the workhouse. I feel I'm really helping people in need,' Daisy wrote, and she'd drawn a smiling face at the end of her letter.

When Alfie went away, Rascal lay by the kitchen door of Faraday House and waited for him to come back. Just like she'd done in the old days when Alfie had gone to school. But this time Alfie didn't come back at night and he still wasn't there in the morning. Rascal kept on waiting.

One day Daisy came to see her. Rascal was wildly excited and ran round and round, checking behind her to see if Alfie was there – but he wasn't. Rascal grabbed her ball from her basket, dropped it at Daisy's feet, wagged her tail and looked up at Alfie's sister. But Daisy wasn't ready to play yet.

'Come on,' she said, clipping Rascal's lead to her purple, white and green collar. There are some friends I want you to meet.'

The children at Sylvia Pankhurst's school in Bow were very excited to meet Rascal and Rascal was very happy to meet them. Her tail wagged and wagged.

'Why's your dog got a purple, white and green collar?' a six-year-old boy called Jack wanted to know.

'It's the colours of the Women's Social and Political Union party,' Daisy told him as she stroked Rascal. 'Purple for dignity, white for purity and green for hope.'

'Would Rascal like to play with my ball?' Jack asked.

Rascal jumped up and wagged her tail as soon as she saw the ball. They went to play in the garden at the back of the toy factory.

'You remind me of my brother Alfie,' Daisy told Jack. 'Rascal's his dog, really, but Alfie's fighting at the front. He misses her terribly.'

'I wish I could have a dog,' Jack said.

Daisy smiled. 'Just like Alfie.'

Before Daisy took Rascal back to Hampton Court, she took her into the toy factory to meet the women working there. Rascal sniffed at the smell of paint that was being painted on the wooden toys and was given a stroke by a lady fixing arms and legs on to dolls. A woman who'd been stuffing a teddy bear looked at Rascal and then quickly started drawing on a piece of paper.

'We don't have a dog toy yet,' she said. 'But it wouldn't be so different from making a teddy bear, and Rascal's the perfect model!'

Manna wrote to tell Alfie that the princess had taken Rascal with her to visit the wounded Indian soldiers who were now in hospital at the Brighton Pavilion.

'She said Rascal was extremely well behaved and the soldiers very much enjoyed meeting her in the grounds of the hospital.'

Often Alfie dreamed that he heard Rascal barking, and he'd open his eyes ready to jump up and see what was wrong, but then he'd remember she wasn't with him. She was back home in England. Safe. Far away from the threat of mustard gas and the enemy. He was very glad about that, although he wished she was with him every day. Not just because he missed her terribly but because of the rat problem. Rats were everywhere in the trenches and if you felt something tickling your face late at night, like as not it was one of them.

'One pair of rats can produce nine hundred babies a year,' Tom told him, which didn't help at all.

The best time of the day was when the letters from home were given out.

'Daisy says she's a suffragette,' Tom said one day when he'd read his letter from her.

Alfie nodded. 'I used to be Mrs Pankhurst's messenger boy, with my dog, Rascal,' he told him.

'So that's where I've seen you before!' Tom said, suddenly remembering. 'At Edith Garrud's martial-arts class. That tiny woman took me totally by surprise. One minute I was standing there and the next I was lying on the ground looking up at the ceiling, with no idea what had just happened!'

Alfie laughed. 'I remember that! It was the first time I met Mrs Garrud – fierce lady!'

'Didn't look like she'd put up with any nonsense,' Tom agreed.

'My sister Daisy was the one who helped you up,' Alfie said.

'Oh, so *that* was your Daisy,' Tom said, and he gave a smile as he shook his head. 'Small world.'

'Daisy was one of Mrs Pankhurst's Amazons,' Alfie told him.

They'd read in the newspapers that were brought over from England how Mrs Pankhurst had been to Russia and met the soldiers of the Women's Battalion of Death unit, who were off to fight at the front for their country.

'I bet Daisy would have joined that if she could,' Alfie said, and Tom nodded.

But they were both secretly glad that she couldn't.

'Wouldn't wish going to war on anyone,' Tom said.

'No,' Alfie agreed. He was very glad that Manna still hadn't reached the regulation five feet three inches.

It was not until 1918, on the eleventh hour of the eleventh day of the eleventh month, that the fighting was finally over. Alfie was desperately looking forward to seeing Rascal again. Four long years of war had kept him apart from his best friend.

When he and Tom got off the train at the station, he was overjoyed to see Daisy and Mrs Pankhurst waiting for them.

'Where's Rascal and Manna?' he asked. He'd told Tom so much about Rascal that he couldn't wait for him to meet her.

'We're going in the car to see them,' Mrs Pankhurst told them as Alfie and Tom put their kit bags in the boot.

When they got to Faraday House, Alfie saw Rascal lying on the lawn in the sunshine being stroked by Manna. There were three puppies that looked a lot like her and a bit like Princess Sophia's Pomeranians playing together close by.

'Rascal!' Alfie said softly.

It was loud enough for Rascal to hear. She looked over at the visitors and then did a double take and gave a yelp of pure joy when she saw Alfie. She'd waited for him for so long. The next moment she'd scrambled to her feet and was racing over to him. She leapt into his arms, almost knocking him over, and licked and licked his face.

Alfie could feel her heart beating very fast and she made happy little crying sounds.

'I'll never go away again,' he promised.

The three puppies came running over too, wanting to know what their mum was doing and what all the fuss was about.

Alfie knelt down to say hello to them all while still stroking Rascal.

'Fancy you being a mummy dog now,' he said, as the three puppies crawled into his lap and he pressed his face to Rascal's. 'I bet you're a very good mum.'

'All of us were very surprised when she had puppies,' Manna said. 'What are you going to name them? There's one boy and two girls.'

Alfie looked over at Mrs Pankhurst and knew exactly what the puppies should be called.

'The little boy I'm naming Harry,' he said, and Mrs Pankhurst gasped. 'And the little girls should be Mary and Emily.'

Now Mrs Pankhurst was nodding.

'Thank you, Alfie,' she said softly. 'They are beautiful names.'

Rascal came over to Mrs Pankhurst and she gave her a stroke. 'Look at you, all grown up with a family of your own,' she said. 'It seems like no time at all since you were a little pup.'

'Hello, Rascal,' Tom said, crouching down to greet her.

Rascal sniffed at him, wagged her tail, gave one of her distinctive Staffie grins, ran into a nearby bush, came out with a ball, dropped it at his feet and looked up at him with her head tilted to one side.

'Looks like you have her approval,' Daisy said with a smile.

'We've met before,' Tom told her.

A few months later the law was changed. Women aged over thirty who owned property were given the right to vote. This right was also given to all men over twenty-one, or over nineteen if they'd been in the war.

'So you'll be able to vote too now, Alfie,' Daisy told him.

'You did it!' Alfie congratulated Mrs Pankhurst.

But Mrs Pankhurst said it was only the beginning. 'One day I want all men and women to have equal rights.'

And Alfie was sure, if anyone could make it happen, it was Emmeline Pankhurst.

Glossary

Ada Wright: one of the suffragettes who took part in the Black Friday protest outside Parliament on 18 November 1910.

Adela Pankhurst (19 June 1885–23 May 1961): third daughter of Emmeline Pankhurst, suffragette and political activist, who moved to Australia in 1914.

Annie Kenney (13 September 1879– 9 July 1953): suffragette from a poor family, who started work in a cotton mill in Yorkshire at the age of ten. She was one of the first suffragettes to be imprisoned, in 1905, for demanding women's right to vote at a political rally in Manchester. She became deputy leader of the Women's Social and Political Union (WSPU) in 1912.

Bodyguard unit: the WSPU trained thirty women in martial arts and self-defence to protect suffragettes from re-arrest under the Cat and Mouse Act. Newspaper reports called them the 'Jiujitsuffragettes' and the 'Amazons'.

Bryant and May: British company which made matches. In the nineteenth century, its factory in the East End of London employed mostly women and teenage girls, who worked fourteen-hour days in bad conditions and for very little money. The match girls' strike of 1888 led to better working conditions.

Cat and Mouse Act: popular name for the Prisoners (Temporary Discharge for Ill

Health) Act, 1913. It meant that suffragettes who went on hunger strike in prison were released when they became sick. When they got better, they were taken back to prison to finish their sentences.

Caxton Hall, Westminster: public hall used by the WSPU from 1907 to hold a 'Women's Parliament' each year, followed by a procession to the Houses of Parliament to present a petition to the prime minister.

Christabel Pankhurst (22 September 1880–13 February 1958): oldest daughter of Emmeline Pankhurst; together they founded the WSPU in 1903. From 1912 to 1913 Christabel directed the WSPU from exile in France.

David Lloyd George (17 January 1863–26 March 1945): Chancellor of the Exchequer (the minister responsible for deciding how much money the government can spend) from 1908 to 1915 in Asquith's government. He went on to become prime minister (6 December 1916–19 October 1922).

Derby: horserace at Epsom Downs Racecourse in Surrey, run on the first Wednesday in June from 1900 to 1995. The horses race 1.5 miles on flat grass without jumps. During the time that this story is set, it was extremely popular and an unofficial holiday.

dojo: room or hall in which judo and other martial arts are practised.

Dr Flora Murray (8 May 1869–28 July 1923): Scottish medical pioneer and member of the WSPU. She looked after Emmeline Pankhurst and other hunger strikers after their release from prison. With Louisa Garrett Anderson she founded the Women's Hospital for Children in west London, to provide health care for working-class children.

Dr Louisa Garrett Anderson (1873–1943): medical pioneer, member of the WSPU and social reformer.

East End: poor area of London, east of the City, the financial district.

Edith Margaret Garrud (1872–1971): one of the first female teachers of martial arts in the Western world. She trained the bodyguard unit of the WSPU in jiu-jitsu.

Emily Wilding Davison (1872–1913): key member of the WSPU. She was killed in a protest action at the Epsom Derby.

Emmeline Pankhurst (15 July 1858–14 June 1928): political activist and leader of the British suffragette movement, who helped women win the right to vote. In 1889 she founded the Women's Franchise League, which fought to allow married women to vote in local elections. In October 1903 she helped found the more militant

WSPU. With the outbreak of war in 1914, she supported the government's war effort.

Ernestine Mills: one of the suffragettes who took part in the Black Friday protest outside Parliament; she was knocked to the ground by police and photographed, shielding her face, by a journalist from the *Daily Mirror*. An artist and metalworker, she made jewellery for the WSPU.

Ethel Smyth (22 April 1858–8 May 1944): composer and suffragette. Her song, 'The March of the Women', became the anthem of the WSPU.

Evelina Haverfield (1867–1920): suffragette and aid worker, who was arrested several times for obstructing the police during WSPU protests. She was a member of the cycling suffragettes and named her bicycle Pegasus. At the start of the First

World War, she founded the Women's Emergency Corps.

Faraday House, Hampton Court Green: house in Hampton Court Road, East Molesey. The English scientist Michael Faraday lived there from 1858 to 1865. It became the home of Princess Sophia Duleep Singh.

Flora Drummond (1878–1949): known as The General, she was an inspiring public speaker and organizer for the WSPU, imprisoned nine times for her protests.

Hampton Court Palace: royal palace on the River Thames in south-west London, dating from 1515 and lived in by kings and queens from Henry VIII to George II.

Harry Pankhurst (1889–1910): youngest child of Emmeline Pankhurst, who died aged twenty-one.

Herbert and Laura Goulden: Emmeline Pankhurst's younger brother and his wife.

Laura was the first headmistress of Hazelwood School in Palmers Green, North London.

Herbert Henry Asquith (12 September 1852–15 February 1928): prime minister of the United Kingdom from 1908 to 1916, who opposed women's right to vote.

Hilda Brackenbury (27 April 1832–October 1918): suffragette and supporter of the WSPU. She and her daughters Georgina and Marie were arrested for smashing windows in the West End of London in 1912. Her home, 2 Campden Hill Square, offered members of the WSPU a place to recover when they were released from prison.

Houses of Parliament: the Palace of Westminster in London, the seat of the two houses of the Parliament of the United Kingdom: the House of Commons and the House of Lords.

hunger strike: refusing to eat as an act of political protest. Many suffragettes went on hunger strike in prison and they were often force-fed. In 1913 the government replaced force-feeding with the Cat and Mouse Act.

jiu-jitsu: Japanese system of unarmed combat and physical training.

kettling: police tactic of keeping a group of protesters in a small area during a protest.

Lincoln's Inn House: the WSPU moved into its new headquarters on Kingsway, London, in the summer of 1912. On 30 April 1913 it was raided by the police.

Maharajah Ranjit Singh (1780–1839): ruler of the Sikh empire in north-western India and grandfather of Princess Sophia Duleep Singh.

Mary Jane Clarke (1862–1910): suffragette and younger sister of Emmeline Pankhurst.

She was arrested for smashing windows on 23 November 1910 and went on hunger strike in Holloway prison. She died three days after being released.

number 10 Downing Street: official home of the prime minister.

omnibus: the first buses to be used in London, from 1829, were horse-drawn vehicles; motor omnibuses were introduced in 1902.

Parliament: law-making body of the United Kingdom, made up of the House of Commons and the House of Lords.

Parliamentary bill: idea for a new law that is presented in Parliament. If the bill is approved by the House of Commons, House of Lords and the monarch, it becomes an Act of Parliament and is law.

pit brow: worker, usually female, employed to sort coal at the edge of a coalmine.

Poor Law Guardian: someone who helped to administer the Poor Law and ensure a workhouse was run correctly.

Princess Sophia Alexandra Duleep Singh (8 August 1876–22 August 1948): daughter of Duleep Singh, Maharajah of the Punjab, and god-daughter of Queen Victoria. A leading suffragette, she was fined for refusing to pay taxes; she campaigned for equality and justice in both England and India.

road apples: horse droppings

Rosa May Billinghurst (1875–1953): suffragette who was paralysed from the waist down as a child and used a tricycle wheelchair for mobility; she was arrested several times for her part in WSPU protests.

St Stephen's Entrance: public entrance to the Houses of Parliament, also known as the Strangers' Entrance.

Strangers' Gallery: members of the public can enter the Houses of Parliament and watch what's going on in the House of Commons from this area, now known as the Visitors' Gallery. The term 'strangers' referred to people who were not members of Parliament or staff.

suffrage: right to vote in political elections, also known as the franchise.

suffrage movement: the fact that only wealthy landowners could vote to elect members of Parliament came to be seen as unfair and the belief that everyone should have the right to vote grew throughout the nineteenth century. The 1884 Reform Act allowed more people to vote, but all women and the poorest 40 per cent of adult males were still not allowed to. The 1918 Representation of the People Act gave the vote to all men over twenty-one and to women over the age of thirty who owned a certain amount of property. The Equal Franchise Act of 1928 gave equal voting rights to women and men, from the age of twenty-one, with no property restrictions.

suffragette: woman seeking the right to vote through organized protest, particularly a member of a militant organization such as the WSPU. Campaigners who used non-violent tactics were known as suffragists.

Sylvia Pankhurst (5 May 1882– 27 September 1960): second daughter of Emmeline Pankhurst, a leader of the WSPU and supporter of workers' rights.

Votes for Women: campaign slogan of the suffragettes and title of the WSPU newspaper from 1907 to 1912. The WSPU newspaper was later called *The Suffragette*.

water fountain in Parliament Square Garden: the Buxton Memorial Fountain was built in 1866 to celebrate the emancipation of slaves in the British Empire in 1834.

Winston Churchill (30 November 1874– 24 January 1965): Home Secretary in Asquith's government from 19 February 1910 to 24 October 1911 and responsible for policing and prisons. He went on to serve twice as prime minister: from 1940 to 1945, leading Britain to victory over Nazi Germany during the Second World War, and again from 1951 to 1955.

Women's Freedom League: group campaigning for women's suffrage and equality. It was founded in 1907 by seventy members of the WSPU who supported non-violent protest.

Women's Social and Political Union (WSPU): main militant organization campaigning for women's right to vote in the United Kingdom from 1903 to 1917, led by Emmeline Pankhurst and her daughters Christabel and Sylvia. Its members, known as 'suffragettes', adopted the slogan 'Deeds not Words', because they believed the best way to win the vote was through direct political action, such as breaking windows, setting fire to unoccupied buildings and going on hunger strike when arrested and imprisoned.

workhouse: public institution that provided the poor people of a parish with board and lodging in return for work.

Acknowledgements

The research for this book has involved meeting and getting to know many wonderful, amazing and helpful people and animals. When *Emmeline and the Plucky Pup* was first commissioned I was in Manchester and able to visit the museum of Mrs Pankhurst's home, now situated within the grounds of Manchester Royal Infirmary. The staff and volunteers there were both very welcoming and informative and I knew I wanted to start my story there.

I've been interested in martial arts since I was a child and trained briefly both in the UK and abroad (not that that means I'm particularly adept!). I found *Sensei* and suffragette Edith Garrud and her training of Mrs Pankhurst's bodyguards, known as 'the Amazons', in jiu-jitsu fascinating. My local jiu-jitsu club was extremely helpful when I went along as part of my research and I'd especially like to thank Sensei Keith Cooper, who not only showed me how to get out of a stranglehold but also how the suffragettes would have been taught to fight using sticks. At an afternoon event I learnt about how the police use martial arts now (and over the course of the last century) from DC Tredwell, watching in awe as Rosi Sexton demonstrated that physical size holds no limitations for a talented Brazilian jiu-jitsuist.

When it came to writing this book it was my pleasure to work once again with editor Carmen McCullough, who commissioned it, with wonderful Mainga Bhima for the drafts that followed through to completion and Emma Jones for the very last part. Copy-editors Daphne Tagg and Frances Evans did their jobs brilliantly, and proofreaders Sarah Hall and Susi Elmer were supremely meticulous – which I'm very grateful for. The cover for the book is just stunning, especially dear little Rascal, and I'd like to thank illustrator Angelo Rinaldi and designer Jan Bielecki. On the PR and Marketing side of things I feel very lucky to have been able to work with Jasmine Joynson and Lucie Sharpe who've also been part of the book tours and are loved by my dogs, Bella and Freya. Sales experts Tineke Mollemans and Kirsty Bradbury have been with me throughout the writing of all my Megan Rix books and a huge support. Not forgetting my long-time agent and friend Clare Pearson of Eddison Pearson. Thank you.

Having the support of my family makes such a difference and as always I'd like to thank my husband, Eric, who ends up knowing almost more about whatever topic I'm writing on than I do! Sharing an office with him has increased my productivity no end. He also kindly visited the fascinating Workhouse Museum – and took some stunning photographs – when I was unable to go plus he found the vintage photographs of pet dogs living in workhouses, which led to Sniffer's inclusion in the story. As well as solving the query over the colour of Flora Drummond's military coat using black-and-white to colour photography software. ☺

Finally, my own dogs, golden retrievers Traffy, Bella and Freya, have been and are a continual source of inspiration and fun. They put up with shorter walks while I was in the midst of writing this book and enjoyed much longer ones when I wasn't. Bella and Freya have been attending dog training classes at 'Happy Dogs' since they were tiny pups and during the writing of this book their trainer, Laura Foster, brought a lively, noisy, funny and utterly adorable Parson Jack Russell terrier puppy called Colin to the classes. Colin helped inspire the character of Rascal when she was a tiny pup, as did the other dogs and puppies that my own dogs have met over the years. When Traffy was still very young her best friend was a little Staffie puppy called Jelly, who used to have the most adorable sulks where he would curl up and not look at his 'mum' when he was asked to do something he didn't want to. Recently, Bella's been helping to teach a two-year-old Staffie called Daisy to grow more confident in the river. Daisy loves playing with her ball in the water but was nervous of bringing it back when she got out of her depth. Bella would swim out and fetch the ball for her and drop it next to Daisy, who'd then run up the riverbank with it ready for the ball to be thrown again. The river itself and the woods around it are forever changing on our walks throughout the year when we'll see foxes, deer, badgers, cormorants, herons, kingfishers and even otters at different times. I find it an unending source of writing inspiration as well as the perfect place to reflect and plan future books. ☺

If you've enjoyed Emmeline's adventures with Rascal, you'll love reading about Little Houdini, the kitten who's destined to be a birthday present for Winston Churchill!

Turn the page to meet him . . .

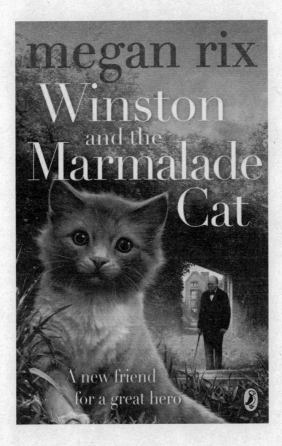

Chapter 1

The small kitten raced across the icy wasteland after his prey, but the yellow autumn leaf was held by the wind and flew just ahead of him, out of reach of the kitten's paws.

Determined not to lose it, the kitten ran on, leaving the den where his mother and his brothers and sisters still slept far behind.

When the wind finally released the leaf and it dropped to the ground, the kitten pounced on it with a crunch and stared down at his prey, triumphant. Then he spotted another leaf dancing in the wind, another leaf that needed to be caught before it could escape. He released the first one to dash after the second, but then another leaf fell to the side of him and he darted after that instead.

Sometimes he jumped up to catch the fleeing leaves mid-air. Sometimes he pounced on them when they hit the ground, but there were too many crisp late November leaves for one small kitten to be able to catch them all.

The kitten looked back again at the hawthorn bush that his family was hidden in and gave a miaow, but none of them came to help.

He watched as a sparrow flew above him, then spied a worm that disappeared back below the ground before the hungry kitten could reach it.

In front of him, the kitten spied a long, thin metal tunnel lying on the ground. When he poked his head inside it he saw a mouse on the grass at the other end. The kitten's heart beat fast with excitement and he crouched low as he squeezed into the tunnel and headed towards it.

A moment later the kitten gave a cry as the tunnel lifted off the ground. He slid forward and was covered with thick, black wet mud that stung his eyes. He tried to cry out again but the mud went into his mouth and made him cough.

Worst of all came a great clang followed by a terrifying roar.

The kitten trembled as the roar turned into a juddering hum, and he curled up into a muddy ball in the darkness.

Alone and very afraid.

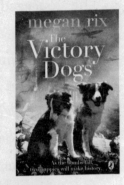
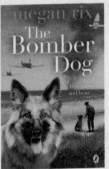
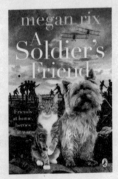